The Prospects Are Pleasing

The Prospects Are Pleasing

a novel by

Honor Tracy

Random House : *New York*

TO CHRISTO GORE-GRIMES

The Prospects Are Pleasing

one

In dead silence the Bombardier paced along the mole of Dun Laoghaire Harbor, looking neither to right nor to left. His young companions respected him too much to open their mouths until he should choose to speak. There were, for the younger of the two at least, excitement and a sense of adventure in merely walking beside this powerful and mysterious man: a man whose real name it was forbidden to know, but whose remarkable appearance drew glances from all who went by. No one who saw the Bombardier could fail to realize that his paths lay outside and beyond those of the common herd.

It was the fine afternoon of a Sunday in April. Far away to the left lay Dublin sprawling in a pool of misty light, with a strange air of unreality as if painted on canvas. Behind them were the spires and trees and terraces of the little harbor town. Milky clouds went scudding over the sky, and the waves tossed and fretted the sailing boats at anchor in the bay. Sea gulls circled and swooped overhead, crying like children; and when they came near, the young men noted, the Bombardier would pause and tilt his head as if trying to understand their plaintive message. At such times his face would take on an entirely new expression, a curious mingling of apprehension and fury.

Of his companions the elder, Liam Mac Lamh, was twenty-five years old, tall and well proportioned, with good looks of a traditionally Irish kind: the hazel eyes and long black lashes, the dazzling smile and the dimples, suggested an actor, idol of matron and adolescent alike. The younger, Thomas O'Driscoll, was less favored, with his red curls and narrow shoulders, but there was an intensity about him, an air as of quiet desperation, which made him appear the more interesting personality of the two. He owed this quality to lack of food, exercise and sleep, but it made, none the less, a striking impression.

At last, having reached the end of the long mole, the Bombardier halted and turned his great smoldering eyes in the direction of the British coast. For a while he stood thus, his lips moving in private imprecation; and then, heaving a sigh that was almost a groan, he addressed them.

"Are the instructions perfectly clear?" he asked in his deep, rich voice.

"Oh, they are, Bombardier, they are," promptly answered the two of them in chorus.

"Anything in the plan seem doubtful?"

"Not at all," they said.

"Depend on us," added Thomas O'Driscoll; "we'll do it if it is humanly possible." He spoke with a slight stammer.

"Here, then, are ten pounds for each of you. As soon as you have gained your first objective, you will send a wire to 'Cartwright,' care of the Nassau Lounge, saying *The apples are ripe* and signing yourselves 'Painter.' 'Cartwright' then will wire further funds to 'Painter' care of the Piccadilly Post Office; these will enable you to complete the mission."

Again he fell silent for a space, brooding.

"May God have you in His keeping," he said next, with much earnestness of manner. "Be very sure, if you succeed, that the Organization will know how to show its gratitude."

It was indeed a grave matter that the Bombardier had committed to their young but fervent hands. A grave injustice to Ireland was to be set right by daring and resolute action. Twenty years ago the great Spanish painter Afrodisio Lafuente y Chaos had died and bequeathed to the Morgan Gallery, London, three of the finest canvases of his "Goat" period. He had done this as a gesture to England, "in memory of happy days spent at Yarmouth, Ramsgate and Ballybunion." The full implications of this had not immediately struck the minds of the Irish people. Beyond laughing quietly at the idea of anyone forgetting where Ballybunion was, they thought nothing of it at the time. It was an English journalist, a Mr. Evelyn Burbage, who recently had drawn their attention to the cruel wrong that was done them.

Mr. Burbage worked for that progressive organ, *The New Dealer,* and he specialized in demonstrating that England was absolutely to blame for all that happened anywhere. On Ireland, a country he had never visited, he had written copiously in the past, and his more imaginative remarks had been widely quoted in the Irish Press as reflecting informed Eng-

lish opinion. Only two years previously he had con-
trived to show that a bug introduced into Ireland by
the English soldiery had brought about the failure
of the potato crop in 1846 and, hence, the Famine;
and after this he had been content to lie fallow
awhile. Now he was back at work, with a trenchant
article demanding that one of the Lafuente canvases
be "returned" at once to "the rightful owners." Legality, he emphasized, was not enough; decency and
justice had claims as well; the "real intentions" of
the legator must be borne in mind—and, with a
moving tribute to the spiritual riches and material
poverty of the Irish nation, he concluded.

Spurred on by informed English opinion, Ireland
had no choice but to play up. Once more Erin's
harp was set a-throbbing with grief; and a small boy
with adenoids telephoned daily to the British Embassy to inform it that the English were all bloody
thieves as well as murderers. Yet even so the affair
might have come quietly to rest if a Dublin editor
had not had the unhappy idea of approaching Sir
Alvary Wilberforce, Director of the Morgan Gallery,
for his view of it. He rang Sir Alvary up at his private house, rather late in the evening; and, after a
great deal of explanation on his part, the fruity voice
across the water declared that its owner had never
heard such a lot of damned tripe in his life, adding
gratuitously and irrelevantly that he had yet to meet
the Irishman who knew an Afrodisio Lafuente from
an El Greco. Naturally, this meant war.

A few weeks later there appeared in a Dublin evening newspaper an advertisement inviting "brave,
strong, resourceful youths interested in justice for
Ireland" to apply to a box number for full particu-
lars as to how this might be obtained. It was thus

that Thomas O'Driscoll, like Liam Mac Lamh, had
come in touch with the Bombardier; and he, with
his magnificent head, his mane of silvery hair and
the strange light that glowed in his eyes whenever
he spoke of their native land, had captured the boy's
imagination entirely. He made Tommy feel he must
prove himself, dare and suffer all things for his sake;
and when after preliminary conversations and swear-
ing to secrecy he revealed that the task he offered,
on the orders of a body he could not discuss, was to
go to London, recover one of the Lafuente canvases
by guile or force and smuggle it over the Irish Sea,
the boy had accepted it at once.

"Anyone of the three will do," the Bombardier had
said. "That's not the important part of it at all."

Now the plans were completed and each of the
boys knew exactly what he had to do. This meeting
had simply been for the purpose of receiving the
Bombardier's last instructions, his blessing and the
money for their fares; tomorrow they were to cross
to England by the evening boat.

The Bombardier pulled out his watch and muttered an exclamation.

"I must leave you lads," he said, with a hint of
testiness in his voice. "As soon as I am halfway up
the pier you, Mac Lamh, follow on. O'Driscoll, after
that. From now on, never be seen together. Do not
recognize each other on the boat. And above all, not
a word of all this to a living soul."

He wheeled about and strode down the pier toward the shore. When he had gone a little way the
clocks of the town could be heard striking five, one
after the other, and he quickened his step until it
almost became a run. What was the deep significance
of the hour? And then again he halted in his tracks

and flung up an arm as if to ward off a blow. What could it mean? There was nothing anywhere near him but the sea gulls overhead. Tommy followed the burly figure's progress with awe in his face.

"I wonder where he's going?" he breathed.

"Hush!" said Liam.

"You are right, of course; it is not for us to speculate."

"Would you say he was halfway along?"

"Not yet."

There was a pause and then Tommy shouted, "Now!"

"Till tomorrow, Tomás."

"Till Tuesday. We know nothing of each other tomorrow."

"Right you are. I can see you were born to this. Good-bye."

As Liam set off in his turn, Tommy stood gazing out to sea in a kind of trance. He could hardly believe the luck that had thrown him in with the Bombardier and in so short a space of time transformed, at least inwardly, the whole of his life. He had always burned to distinguish himself for Ireland's sake, and indeed had begun work on half a dozen plays that were to establish him as the new Bernard Shaw. Yet somehow or other he was never able to finish them, nor was he sure they would have the desired result if he could. When he read over in cold daylight what he had written with so much fervor the evening before, it seemed to him that he might have some little way to go. If his mother could have paid for the training he would have become a great doctor; he would have been one of those Dublin giants whom, he understood, the big men in London were always sending for in a hurry. As it was, he worked in the showroom of Kitchen Accessories, Ltd. He would have joined the Irish Republican Army, but hesitated, lest he fall into mortal sin or lose his job; and, also, because he liked his spare time to himself.

Then came the great day of the Bombardier's advertisement.

In the ordinary way it took Tommy two weeks at least to bring himself to write a letter, and even then he usually forgot to post it. Now he sat down and fluently answered the call without a moment's delay. He had expatiated on his strength, bravery and resource, citing a number of imaginary episodes in support of these, and as for justice to Ireland, he declared himself willing to give up his life if it would help matters forward. His father had died when he was a baby, worn out by the struggle for Irish freedom; his mother was a native Irish speaker; and he asked no more than to be worthy of them, remaining, yours respectfully, Thomas O'Driscoll.

Remembering this letter now as he began to walk back to the shore, Tommy quite believed in it. To be sure, he could have expressed certain things differently; he could with perfect propriety have said, for example, that his father had been run over. But it seemed to him that his duty was to give a true impression rather than simply to record the facts as such. His father had undoubtedly been concerned in the national movement, and if not actually in the Post Office during the siege of 1916, was given a job there later; and when the accident occurred in 1943, he could only have been worrying so much about Ireland that he failed to see the bus in time. Again, it might loosely be stated that his mother was born and reared in England and knew not a word of Irish; but he would be a very bad son if he mentioned anything so disgraceful, and she had, after all, on the death of her husband retired to a cabin in the Gaeltacht. As for his own deeds of daring, he was quite simply looking into the future and describing what he saw there. He could see no harm at all in that.

When he reached the town and mingled again with the people going about their dull occasions, he looked at them with new eyes—eyes that were full of love, the eyes of a dedicated man. He felt in a strange, sweet way that he was set apart from them by virtue of the perils and hardships that he must undergo for their sake. He was the Anointed, the Victim and, at the same time, the Hero. And in a marvelous way his whole inner life was strengthened and cleansed. As a rule, when he gave rein to his fancy, there was always an imaginary audience: he performed his deeds of valor or achieved his triumphs in art before ghostly witnesses who were stunned with admiration. He would construct in his mind prolix, laudatory discussions of himself and his doings by perfect strangers.

"Do you know what I adore about that fellow O'Driscoll?" he would hear one voice say to another. Or, "I never saw such brilliance. Honest to God, the man's a miracle."

Now the invisible spectators were gone, the phantom applause was hushed; there was nothing to mar the purity of his aim and the strength of his resolution. And then again, as he took the bus that should bring him home, this commonplace act that he performed every day of his life brought him a sudden, overwhelming sense of unreality. For a moment he thought he was in a dream. I am going to London to get our picture from the English, he whispered, as a little boy might whisper, Tomorrow is Christmas Day. Yet he still could not believe it, although the medical certificate of his unfitness for work, signed by his friend McGrath, was in the post to Kitchen Accessories. It was not until his hand, groping for the bus fare, came in contact with the notes provided by the Bombardier, that his soul caught fire again. There was nothing hallucinatory about them at any rate: ten pounds were ten pounds.

Now he fell to musing on the confidence the Bombardier had shown in him. A fine judge of character he must be, for there was many a fellow would blow the lot and let the mission go hang. Prepared as he was to die for Ireland, Tommy yet had no opinion at all of the Irish. The Bombardier knew nothing about him but his name; at his desire, all correspondence between them had been carried on through accommodation addresses, with a certain amount of inconvenience to both. He had asked for no receipt for the money. It was rarely that Thomas O'Driscoll held ten pounds in his hand at the one time, but he was not tempted in the slightest degree; and as he told himself so, his eye moistened and his bosom swelled with pride.

"I declare, the fellow's in a trance!"

Tommy looked confusedly up to find the conductor standing beside him with arms akimbo and a professionally humorous look on his face. The bus had stopped, and all the passengers were laughing.

"Is . . . is this Ballyknock?" he stammered; and there was another ripple of amusement.

"Well now," the conductor said, peering through the window with exaggerated interest, "I'd say it was. It looks like Ballyknock all right. It *says* Ballyknock on the board. But there may be some error."

"I want no impertinence," the patriot said, rising loftily and tripping over his raincoat.

"Ah, sure, I'm to blame," the man riposted, throwing a look around his audience. "You were looking for us to bring you to your door, and we've suspended the taxi service on Sundays. I forgot to mention it."

Tommy dealt him a look of frigid contempt and made his way down the bus as calmly and importantly as he could. Titters arose on every side as he hooked his sleeve on the door handle and had to be freed by the smiling conductor. He felt jarred in his soul as he walked slowly down the hill and across the river to the great barn of a house where he lived. It was remarkable, too, that the nearer he came to this house the more his whole demeanor changed. He crept up to the front door with the furtive air of a felon rather than with the bold pace of the hero he was shortly to be. Having shut it behind him as softly as he could, he paused in the corridor and listened intently. Next he crept to the foot of the stairs and listened again, as much to the pounding of his heart as to anything else. Now he went up, noiselessly putting his feet down one after the other. Gently he turned the handle of his own door, he squeezed inside and shut it, he leaned against it in an attitude of exhaustion and relief, and, wiping his forehead, he exclaimed aloud, "Thanks be to God, she's out!"

Far above his head, speaking as it were from Heaven itself, a merry voice replied, "Who is? The Cat's Mother?"

two

The house in which Tommy had what he described as his furnished apartments had been a rectory in the heyday of the Protestant ascendency. The present Landlord had bought it because she liked having plenty of room, both for herself to turn round in and also to rent, in the shape of flats, to interesting people. It was her dream to found, here in this quiet little village, a colony of writers, artists and thinkers. Despite the abundance of these in Ireland, so far she had not been entirely successful; and further, thanks to her unshakable belief that she had only to look a person once in the eyes to assess his character fully, and to her own custom of believing implicitly what people told her about themselves, she had assembled at one time and another as fine a collection of detrimentals as could be imagined. They caused her endless amusement, however, and she continued to think of herself as a keen businesswoman.

At the moment Tommy was the only tenant she had. He camped in one corner of an immense, blue-washed attic where there was a bed, a gas ring, a frying pan, a cup, plate and saucer, one fork and two knives, a basket armchair that leaned a little to one side, a looking glass that made things out rather larger than life, three paintings of horses and hounds, and a statue of the Buddha with a price label gummed on its back. Beyond his own concession, which he was able to curtain off at will, the attic was a repository for treasure acquired by the Landlord at auctions. Among them were lacquered screens and golf clubs, a sedan chair, four samovars, a warming pan or two, a suit of Toledo armor, a harp and a stuffed polar bear; all of which, the Landlord believed, must some day come in very handy.

Tommy had joined the household a year or so before. He told her at their preliminary interview that he wrote plays, one of which, his agent informed him, was considered for London production. She treated him to one of her shrewd, penetrating glances and a brisk, satisfied nod of her head. He went on to explain that for the time being his circumstances were straitened, and that the need to live where he could write in peace, away from the roar and whirl of Dublin, would mean a substantial outlay in bus fares. With her quick sympathy for the struggling artist, the Landlord had declared she had just the thing and had offered him this, which she called the Bijou, at a nominal rent. He had paid up for a month or so and then got out of the way of it, partly from a temperamental inertia in such affairs, partly from an obscure resentment at the modesty of the figure she had named, reassuring himself with the idea that if she really wanted it she would ask.

It was this state of things that was the cause of his trepidation now. Of late he had begun to fancy he saw a change in her manner toward him: a change of the sort that, hypersensitive as he was, he was wont to suspect in the people, and notably in creditors or employers, associated with him. He thought that this change had some reference to the money he owed; he sensed that a disagreeable exchange of views could not be far away. The thought of anything so sordid on the eve of his great adventure distressed him immeasurably, the more so as there could be no question of back payments now.

The realization, then, that the Landlord was not out after all but somewhere in this crowded room with him was most unnerving, particularly as she was nowhere to be seen. He peered apprehensively this way and that in search of her tiny figure, but could make nothing out beyond the familiar shapes of her possessions. To add to his discomfiture her words were followed by a shriek of laughter, somewhat like the cry of a startled jay.

"You'll have come about the rent, of course," he said, addressing the room at large with what dignity he could muster.

"Hang the old rent!" the voice retorted with another gleeful outburst.

"Where are you, at all?" he inquired crossly.

"Look upwards, angel!"

He turned his eyes in the direction of the voice and gave a cry of alarm. Suspended from two great hooks in the ceiling was a naval hammock, a foot or two below the ceiling itself, on which, comfortably reclined on her back and surrounded by pots and brushes, the Landlord was busily painting a nautical scene.

"I'm cheering the place up a bit," she explained.

"You'll break your back," he warned her. "You're not safe there a bit."

"And who wants to be safe, you softy?"

"How in the Name of God did you get up to it?"

The Landlord did not deign to reply, but stabbed with her brush toward a rope hanging slackly from one of the hooks. She was a keen amateur climber, whether of walls, roofs, drain pipes or trees; and she was never happier than when scampering about the ancient roof with a bucket of tar.

"You should have been a burglar," he told her, amused in spite of himself.

"Hold your row, till I finish this wave." She painted swiftly for a moment or two. "A piece of luck, those hooks being there," she commented. "A hammock is much more handy than a scaffolding, which I'll need for the rest of it. It's going to be the Battle of Trafalgar."

This was the kind of thing that Tommy never allowed to pass.

"Could you not have found an Irish subject?" he asked with quiet reproach.

"I could, of course," the Landlord agreed, "but I didn't, so there. You old Sinn Fein wallah."

"I am a patriot, Mrs. Barry."

"You are in me eye!" she told him, chuckling. "And save us from patriots!"

The genial disparagement in her tone was deeply wounding to him. It was all of a piece with that twinkle in her eye when it rested on him nowadays. And since apparently the rent was not a consideration with her, he was entirely at a loss to explain it. Some-one, he thought, must have poisoned her mind. De-

spite the orders he had received, he threw all discretion away.

"I am so, and I'll prove it," he cried. "Tomorrow
I leave for England on a delicate and dangerous
mission. You may never see me again."

A little round head—capped with the maroon ve-
lour helmet which Mrs. Barry invariably wore for
painting in winter, exchanging it on the first of
every May for a similar model in straw—now came
into view and a pair of bright, laughing eyes surveyed him over the edge of the hammock.

"The only delicate, dangerous mission I'd entrust
you with," she declared, "would be stealing a baby's
milk."

"Mrs. Barry, how can you? What do you know of
me, really? The time is fast approaching when you
will remember these words with pain."

"Hoo hoo hoo! Hoo hoo hoo!" It sounded as if a
whole nest of jays had been suddenly put to flight.

Scarlet in the face, Tommy opened his mouth to
tell her about the Bombardier and the painting and
Liam and his intention of dying if need be; but before he could do so a hoarse voice was heard from
the garden below, uplifted in song.

"Ah, there's Peadar. I want a word with that one!"
and, sticking her brush in her mouth, the Landlord
slid down the ropes with amazing agility, whizzed
over the room like a bullet and shot down the stairs.
"May the divil fly off with you!" she could be heard
shrieking below. "What do you think I pay you for?"

"Ah, wait now, ma'am . . ." came the plaintive
rejoinder.

"Where were you all afternoon till now? In the
pub, I'm sure."

"A lady like yourself wouldn't know it," Peadar gently chided her, "but them places don't open till five on a Sunday. It's true for you all right, I was there one poor little minute to ease the dryness; but I was out of it again before you'd boil an egg."

Glowering, Tommy listened to the battle as its fury gradually mounted. Mrs. Barry's relations with her gardener and handyman always caused him intense irritation. To his way of thinking, Peadar was the perfect stage Irishman, drunken, incompetent, a smooth and beguiling liar, the product of centuries of oppression; and, contrary to all appearance, his employer loved him dearly. As a member of the former ascendency, she ought to have despised the creature, and this Tommy would keenly and enjoyably have resented on his behalf; but while she harried him without mercy herself, no one else dared utter a word against him. It was incomprehensible.

"I never saw such a fool in my life" came now in her carrying voice. "The bonfire you lit destroyed a whole bed of seedlings."

"God help me, woman dear, I haven't your brains."

"And why in the name of glory paint the wheel-barrow red?"

"Hadn't I a half-pot of the red going spare?" Peadar inquired. "And weren't you scalding me the other day for letting paint go waste, and the place so shabby?"

Tommy stalked across the attic into the Bijou and drew the curtains around it with the air of a magician enveloping himself in a cloud. Peadar's eternal clowning filled him with disgust; he hardly seemed a person at all, rather a phantom strayed from the Abbey Theatre. And Ireland was crowded with

phantoms like these, all scratching and nibbling at
the beautiful reality which was none the less beautiful or real for being apparent to so very few. Sometimes at the week end Tommy would make an expedition to Shaw's cottage at Dalkey. He would
climb those stone steps up the hill with the fervor
of a pilgrim and, standing before the squat little
villa, would murmur aloud the great man's message
on the plaque outside: The men of Ireland are mortal and temporal, but her hills are eternal. . . . His
eyes would fill with tears as he murmured. Simple
and self-evident like all great truths, it moved him to
the depths of his being; and he drew further inspiration from Shaw's quiet faith, his certainty that, could
he ever find time to leave England, the hills of his
native land would still be in position. And yet there
were those who called the man a materialist! mused
Tommy now, looking out at the lovely shapes of the
Wicklow Mountains.

His eyes moistened in familiar fashion but there
was no time to give himself up to the pleasure of it.
He must write to his mother in her quiet little home
in the west, breaking to her as gently as he could the
news of the strange and hazardous path on which
her only son had set his feet. A simple, manly communication it should be, and one suitable for reading aloud to the neighbors; essential this, for Mrs.
O'Driscoll lived next to a lady whose son was a curate
in Chapelizod and who martyred the district with
her self-importance. Taking pen and paper, he wrote
on his knee:

My dearest Mother,
By the time you read these lines I shall be on my way
to complete a delicate and dangerous mission. I may not

tell you what it is, except that it is undertaken for Ireland. Should I not return, you may perhaps find consolation in the thought that I was the worthy son of my father. I go to what may be my last proud adventure with head carried high, secure in the knowledge that if I fall, others will press forward to take my place.

Your devoted son

He read this through with the corners of his mouth drawing down and a lump in his throat. Then a technical consideration occurred to his mind, namely, that by the time she received it the affair would be settled one way or the other. Letters from Dublin were sent to a small town eight or nine miles from his mother's village. From here, they proceeded by carrier to the village itself and were left in a small sub-office which was also a grocery and licensed bar. Mr. Rooney, the proprietor, was a man leisured enough to take a warm interest in his neighbor's affairs; and he subjected the few letters that came to a process which he described as "sorting" and which never lasted less than a day. Tommy thought it would be cruel to frighten his mother unnecessarily, and he did not wish to incur the expense of a telegram.

He thought hard for a little and then, throwing the first letter away, began on a second:

My dearest Mother,

By the time you read these lines you will have learned of my fate from the papers. Forgive me for not having told you before, but I am a soldier and must obey orders. You may perhaps find consolation in the thought that I was the worthy son of my father. I went to my last proud adventure with my head carried high, secure in the knowledge that others will press forward to take my place.

Your devoted son

P.S.—The men of Ireland are mortal and temporal, but her hills are eternal.

He put the letter in an envelope, sealed it and propped it on the window sill, with a further note: "To be posted in the event of my imprisonment or death." He began to go through his pockets to look for a stamp, but changed his mind, thinking it would be wasted if after all he should return in safety. If he did not, Mrs. Barry in her remorse would surely not grudge the postage. Then he sat down in the basket chair, balancing his weight in the special way he had learned to prevent its throwing him, and stared earnestly at the little packet on the sill. It was a cheap buff-colored envelope, abstracted from the stationery cupboard of Kitchen Accessories, Ltd., and yet perhaps it was a historic document. One day both it and the letter inside might be on view in the National Museum, in high company with the tweed suit that Roger Casement often wore in Dublin, and the boots in which Harry Boland had executed his secret mission to America in the First World War. Generations still unborn might bow their heads before it; and at the very idea he almost broke down.

"As God is my eternal judge . . ." Peadar could be heard whining below the window.

Tommy came out of his dream and pulled himself together. He must eat, for he would need all his strength in London. Slowly he picked up his frying pan and carefully examined it. A number of fragments of black pudding adhered to the bottom but not, he judged, enough to make a scouring really necessary. He was greatly attached to this frying pan of his and dreaded to wear it out. From a greasy packet beside the bed he took out some rashers and laid them across the pan: next he lit the gas ring and put them on to cook; and, having opened a bottle of stout, sat down to wait meanwhile, thinking of Ireland and looking intently at himself in the glass.

three

While great events were shaping themselves in the manner described, great projects, too, were slowly coming to fruition. Some years ago the Government of the day had decided to erect near the Dublin airport a permanent Fair of Irish Industry, at a cost, it was said, of millions. The foundations of the great building were laid and work on the walls had started when the Minister of Industry and Commerce, in a private memorandum to his colleagues, drew attention to the fact that there was nothing like enough Irish industry to fill the half of it. Similarly, the Minister of Finance, in a highly confidential paper to the same quarter, revealed that the money to pay for it was simply not there. Both these documents fell into the hands of the Opposition within a couple of hours of their issue, and a horrible row ensued.

The Government resigned, and to the new one fell the task of determining the building's fate. Had it been

placed elsewhere, they could have left it as it was,
unfinished, a lasting memorial to their opponents'
folly; and after a century or two it might well have
been explained away as an English atrocity. But the
daily arrival at the airport of crowds of foreigners,
all eagerly looking for Irish quaintness and charm,
made this undesirable. It was then suggested that it
might be turned into a monastery, but there were
three large monasteries already within a radius of
ten miles, and plans for a fourth had newly been
completed. In a rousing maiden speech, a young deputy of the Dáil next proposed that it might be used
to enshrine such relics of Ireland's immemorial fight
for freedom as could not find room in the National
Museum. He was cheered to the echo; but an an-
nouncement by the Museum itself, a few days later,
that it had acquired a piece of coconut matting on
which Mr. De Valera was believed to have slipped
while hiding in a country hotel in 1919, indicated
that the field was fairly well covered as it was.

Even as they debated the matter, the scandal of
the Watered Milk came, or rather was dragged, to
light. It was a small domestic affair of no importance,
arising from the fact that a certain chain of creameries
had more customers on its books than milk at its
disposal, and had therefore taken the only course
open to it in the circumstances. Normally the affair
would have been hushed up, with no one a penny the
worse; but a member of the Government had an
interest in the firm, and the Opposition saw that its
clear duty was to demand an inquiry. This dragged
on for days and ended inconclusively, but not before
a great many things unconnected with milk had been
exhumed and half the Government named, to their
detriment. There was nothing for it but a general

election, with the result that the party which had initiated the building now was saddled with it again.

With something of the frenzy of a cornered rat, the new Prime Minister declared that it should be finished at once, cost what it would, and that it was to be a Temple of Art, something along the lines of the Prado in Madrid but with a higher charge for admission. The future of the country lay, if anywhere, in the development of the tourist trade; the slogan he offered, speaking in the excellent French he had acquired as an exile, was *"Du tourisme! encore du tourisme! et toujours du tourisme!"* His supporters received the speech with wild applause, his opponents in a grim silence. He appointed a committee, invited applications for the post of Director and, in a carefully worded statement to the Press, assured the anxious public that it would pay for itself twice over as soon as it got going.

The Chairman of the new Committee—pronounced by its members as Cŏmmĭttēē—was a Mr. Mervyn Roche, known as "Tacky" through his having started life as a bookmaker. His small, close-set eyes, his long nose with its deep nostrils, and the vivid blue of his cheeks gave him a curiously simian look; but he was immensely able as well as active, and those familiar with his past career felt that the destiny of the Irish Prado could not be in better hands. The most vocal of the members was a Miss Philomena Scully, who combined a militant piety with a weakness for brandy to a quite remarkable extent; formerly a librarian, she had drawn the winning horse in the Irish Hospitals' Sweepstake a couple of years before and nowadays sat on various educational or cultural committees. There was, further, Mr. Florence MacMahon, one of Dublin's leading auctioneers, who owned a private collection of water colors; Lady Twomey, the widow of a Birmingham biscuit manufacturer, who had known Sir Alfred Munnings slightly in her youth; that well-known Dublin figure, Seumas Cullen, who exhibited, year after year, the same powerful painting under a different name; and a Mr. Connolly, who once had sketched a little, and now wore saffron tweed. Besides their more obvious qualifications, every one of them possessed that of consanguinity with a Minister.

On the afternoon of the Monday that followed Tommy's meeting with the Bombardier, at the very time indeed that he was putting his things together to go for the England boat, the Committee was discussing a matter of delicacy and importance. They were sitting in one of Tacky's innumerable offices and gazing earnestly at a canvas propped against the wall. It was the work of a rising Irish painter who cherished an ardent love of his country, although preferring to live abroad, and who, on hearing of the new project, had immediately offered this picture as a gift. In Venice, the summer before, it had received a gold medal; at the autumn Salon in Paris the critics were lyrical in praise of it; but Tacky's Committee were unaware of this and their feelings were mixed.

"That picture," Miss Scully declared, closing her eyes with a shiver, "is indecent."

"Can art ever be that?" wondered Lady Twomey. In artistic matters she invariably took the noble line, out of respect for Munnings, and the opposite view to Miss Scully's, for her own satisfaction.

"Oh, Lady Twomey! Look at that Oscar Wilde."

"Who is that Oscar Wilde?" asked Mr. Connolly.

"I am not defending Oscar Wilde as a man," Lady Twomey informed the meeting. "But I would not say that his work was indecent. Surely there is nothing objectionable in *The Importance of Being Earnest?"*

"I'd never dream of going to it," Miss Scully averred, shivering again.

"Then how can you judge?"

Tacky nervously rubbed his hands together. "Ladies, we cannot reopen the Wilde case just now."

"But who is Oscar Wilde?" repeated Mr. Connolly with impatience.

"I will tell you afterwards," said Mr. MacMahon.

"Let us come to the point," Tacky pleaded. "What we have to decide is, do we accept or do we reject this offer, made in all sincerity by a young man who has done much to put Ireland on the map in an artistic kind of way?"

"A man who has been divorced," Miss Scully amplified.

"Ah, Philomena, we couldn't reject the painting on those grounds very well," Mr. MacMahon said coaxingly. "We don't want to get ourselves laughed at."

"There's nothing to laugh at in decent principles," Miss Scully ruled with a sniff. "And anyway, there's no need to reject it for that." She pointed a bony, freckled finger at the canvas. "The thing itself is obscene. It is vile. It's the kind of picture you'd expect to find hanging in Hell."

It was the portrait of a young peasant woman in the later stages of pregnancy, sitting on a rough wooden chair with her hands folded in her lap.

"There is nothing obscene about motherhood, surely," Seumas Cullen bestirred himself to say. Motherhood was the theme of his annual picture and he was not going to have it attacked.

"Motherhood is one thing," Miss Scully retorted. "Sheer animalism is another. And the creature's not even wearing a wedding ring."

"There's no motherhood without a certain amount of animalism, me dear, as any married woman will tell you," Lady Twomey remarked in a deft, unscrupulous blow to the body.

Her words had a powerful effect on the masculine elements of the Committee. The hue of Tacky's mandrill cheeks turned darker. Mr. Florence MacMahon looked at his fingernails and, without rising from his chair, executed a kind of shuffling dance with his feet. Seumas Cullen cleared his throat and tremulously eased his collar, as if he found the temperature of the room oppressive. Mr. Connolly stared down his nose and made a circular movement with his right shoulder.

"A fine thing for a Christian lady to say! And with gentlemen present," snarled Miss Scully.

"I must really call this meeting to order," Tacky mumbled.

"Let us have no more abominations, then," Miss Scully prayed.

"Now, please. We are all Catholics here, I hope," Tacky resumed, with a pious look on his congested features that was lovely to see, "and I hope we shall always be guided by Catholic principles."

"Hear, hear!" barked Seumas Cullen.

"I bet we shall," Lady Twomey observed, with melancholy emphasis.

"On the wedding-ring issue, now," the Chairman continued, "no doubt the artist would agree to paint one in. Or maybe he'd sanction our getting the job done locally, to save the trouble and expense."

"Vandals!" moaned Lady Twomey.

"Ring or no ring, the picture is disgusting and pagan," Miss Scully persisted. "It may be the sort of thing that foreigners like. We must show the world that Ireland knows better."

"We'll be giving a slap in the gob to a man who's trying to help us. We shall hurt his feelings and possibly discourage others. And, ladies and gentlemen, do please bear in mind," Tacky said earnestly, "there's going to be a hell of a lot of room to fill up in that place. Honestly, how it is going to be done I do not know."

"In matters of right and wrong I cannot temporize," Miss Scully informed him.

"Just the fine opinion I'd expect of yourself, Miss Scully!"

"Wait now. There's another aspect to it," Mr. MacMahon began. "We're the Committee all right, and we have the say, but we want to be careful, don't we? We don't want to make the wrong decision for business reasons, and then be criticized in certain quarters, do we?"

"He's right, of course," said Seumas Cullen, with energy. "And I suggest as well that these discussions, whatever the outcome, be kept entirely among ourselves. Let it never be said that certain members of the Committee were more particular than others when it came to the moral issue."

"You may say what you like, for me," Lady Twomey said with a toss of her head. "I've no objection to people knowing the truth, which is that certain people on this Committee don't know art from a pig in a field."

"Please, please!" Tacky reproved her. "Ladies and gentlemen, a new and important point is raised, and one which I confess I had overlooked. There's a great deal in what Mr. MacMahon has said. We don't want to get ourselves talked about; that would never do."

"It depends who does the talking," Lady Twomey observed.

"Exactly!" the Chairman cried with an air of triumph, as if she had made his point for him. "We can't be too careful. Let's take a vote on it. Isn't that the best? Those in favor of rejection, please raise their hands," and he raised his own as he finished speaking. Miss Scully's was up already, and was quickly followed by those of Mr. MacMahon and Seumas Cullen: there was a brief pause, and then, with his usual air of bewilderment, Mr. Connolly slowly lifted his. Lady Twomey, who was rocking to and fro in her chair, compressed her lips and stared at the wall.

"Carried!" said Tacky breezily. "A pity we're not unanimous, but it would be a dull old world if we all thought the same. And it's a great privilege, Lady Twomey, to have an artistic lady like yourself among us, to keep us straight on technical matters. Well, that's all our business for just now. Who's coming round to the Club for a drop of what won't poison them? Miss Scully, are you to be tempted?"

"I don't see why not," answered that lady, and the first gleam of a wintry smile appeared on her face. With one more negative decision to their credit, the Committee dispersed about their various occasions. Mr. Connolly was the last out of the door, inquiring persistently of their retreating backs, "But who is Oscar Wilde?"

Another problem connected with the Irish Prado, and one which dwarfed the rest, was receiving attention at the same time. When An Taoiseach in-

vited applications for the post of Director, the response had been overwhelming. County councilors,
veterinary surgeons, a solicitor-cum-tobacconist in
Ballinasloe, retired justices, and a Christian Brother
who had written a pamphlet entitled *Why All the
Fuss About Art?*—all had expressed a willingness to
serve in this way and a confidence in their ability to
do so. It was an open secret, none the less, that the
only candidate to be taken seriously up to the present time had been Mr. Paul O'Farrell. A man well
known in the world of art, whose reputation ex-
tended to London and Paris, who further possessed
a command of the Irish and a brother in the Senate,
he had all that was needed; and if the malicious
tongues of Dublin sometimes called his standing, taste
or knowledge in question, there was at least no doubt
of the brother. It had been a foregone conclusion that
the post would be his, and the general opinion was
that, with his noble brow and commanding presence, his velvet jacket and his broad-brimmed hat,
he would fill it extremely well.

Within the last few days, however, there had been
a new and surprising development: poor Seán O'Hara
had lost his job in London. Mr. O'Farrell had spent
much of his life abroad, and hence there was a
certain mystery about his career, distinguished as it
was understood to be; but O'Hara was a Dublin lad,
and until his appointment as Art Expert on the British Television had never left his native city. The loss
of that brilliant position had come about in a manner
painful to contemplate. Briefly, Mr. O'Hara had appeared on the screen in no fit condition to be viewed
by respectable British families. The program had to
be hurriedly faded out and an apology made for his
sudden attack of influenza. Still more painful was the

fact that all his previous appointments had been lost in much the same way, and that Dublin now had him on her hands again.

"Ah, the decent man!" people sighed when they heard about it.

Something would have to be done for him, and it would have to be something worthwhile, for Dublin must show the world that she valued her gifted sons if the British did not. In no time at all a rumor went round that An Taoiseach was considering him as an alternative to Mr. O'Farrell.

Mr. O'Farrell was anything but delighted. The appointment was to be made in the following way: An Taoiseach would submit the applications after a preliminary weeding-out to a number of persons in Church and public life and, having informally received their advices, would then make his final decision. Instead, then, of walking easily into a position that he felt himself so eminently fitted to hold, Mr. O'Farrell now saw himself obliged to fight for it. He was under no illusion at all as to what lay ahead. Following the custom of the country he would have to call on An Taoiseach's advisers one by one, ingratiate himself with them and solicit their suffrage, like any mere candidate for the French Academy; and a nice bunch of yahoos they were likely to be. He could not even be sure of his brother being named to the panel.

He was too much a man of the world to allow any of this to appear.

"What a curious people we are, O'Dwyer," he said, laughing, to the friend who came running to bring him the news. "How we do respond, do we not, to the weak, the incompetent, the detrimental! A man need only disgrace himself for us to rally behind him at once. 'Ah, sure, the poor soul, God help him!' It's that fatal softness in our character. And how anything in the nature of real superiority does make us wince! A race of slaves, O'Dwyer, I fear, a race of slaves."

O'Dwyer agreed fully and warmly with every word he said, and raced away to inform those interested that O'Farrell was lepping, fit to be tied.

"And he's a right to be, I'd say," someone remarked. "He's the man for the job and he ought to get it. There's far too much of the other thing in Ireland."

"Ah, wait now, poor O'Hara!"

"Oh, I've nothing at all against O'Hara," the other said hastily. "O'Hara's the best in the world."

"And nothing to back him, mind you. O'Farrell has family money."

"Lives like a prince."

"Some fellow was saying the other day," another man began, "that Seán O'Hara was doing a line with a rich English lady in London there. That will fold up now as well, I suppose."

"Sure, God help him!"

"It's a very sad case, indeed," the first man said.

"Yes, but what is the Government thinking about?" asked O'Dwyer. "The circus hasn't started yet, and they're looking for a ringmaster. I was out there a week or two back, and the walls are only a few feet high."

"They're looking ahead. Thinking in terms of centuries. Building up the country's prestige."

"We've all the prestige in the world as it is," O'Dwyer stated. "And without doing a tap for it either. Ah, it's a queer business. I'd say there was something behind it."

Meanwhile, the subject of their discussion was weaving along up Grafton Street arm in arm with his friend Michael Nolan. This faithful butty had never left his side since he had turned up in Dublin forty-eight hours ago, and together they had visited every house of note in the city. At the fall of night Seán went home to Michael's flat and slept in his clothes on the sofa there until the morning light awoke him and his practiced eye could judge from the sun's position that the doors would be open once more. Then up and out went the pair of them, to resume their tour.

Although they were linked together in this affectionate way, it was now for support rather than from any warmth of feeling. A slow deterioration of mutual regard had been setting in over the past few hours, due, in Michael's opinion, to the fact that Seán was being excessively obstinate and, in Seán's, to the fact that Michael was bent on criticizing and humiliating him. It all arose from the Directorship of the Irish Prado. Michael had told him jubilantly of the rumors concerning himself as the likely man for it and urged him to go in and win; but Seán had pulled his lanky frame up to its full height and flatly refused to apply at all.

"I won't ask for it, then," he had said. "They'll have to offer it to me. I'm not saying I'll decline. But I'll not ask either. I'll not be begging and crawling."

Michael had wheedled and flattered and scolded, but all to no purpose, and his temper was wearing thin. He had eaten nothing at all in the last two days and he was a man who liked his meals; but Seán's only reply to his entreaty that they suspend their tour while he got a chop was to call him the slave of his belly. That was the kind of mood he was in, and it seemed poor thanks for what Michael described to himself as a lifetime of selfless devotion.

"The trouble with you, Seán me lad," he said severely, "is that you drink too much."

"Is that right?" Seán cried, firing up at once. "Well, and look who's talking. Why, you haven't a leg under you! If I wasn't there to shore you up, you'd be on your face."

With that he whipped his arm away and, sure enough, Michael measured his length on the ground.

"I'm not saying I'm dead cold sober," he said with dignity, rolling over and raising himself on his arm. "I've taken a jar or two all right. But wasn't I driven to it? And why? Because I'm worrying about *you?*"

"You are, in my eye!" Seán sneered. "I've been drinking to keep you company, and that's the holy truth. And I'll tell you something, Michael, I was never more ashamed in my life. You're a fine spectacle, lying there on the ground like a sack of potatoes. Oh, I'm going to be a whole lot more careful in my associates from this day on. A man in my position has got to be."

"Your position!" Michael screamed. "You haven't got a position, you drunk!"

Seán quivered with passion from head to foot. "I've stood a lot from you this evening for old time's sake, Michael Nolan," he said in a low, furious voice, "but I permit no man living to call me drunk. Our friendship is at an end; from this hour forth we are strangers."

With that he marched unsteadily off in the direction of St. Stephen's Green, forgetting, in his just indignation, that he had nowhere to spend the night.

four

At about twelve o'clock on the following morning Mr. Felix Horniman was passing the Morgan Gallery in London on the way to his Club in Pall Mall. Up to that moment he had been thinking bitterly about a telegram just received from his aunt, in which she had described his behavior and general comportment in life as "odd." Felix was under no illusion as to the gravity of the charge. "Odd" was the harshest term in his aunt's vocabulary, and was applied to all who did not at once comply with her wishes or who held views that differed in some way from her own. She lived in Torremolinos, where her time was mostly taken up in reviling the Spaniards for their cruelty to animals and in succoring the victims of it; she was forever on the go, bathing the sores on donkeys' backs or spraying insecticides into the startled faces of goats, buying mutton chops for cats and throwing fish back in the sea when the fishermen were looking the other way.

In her last letter she had intimated that it would be "pleasant" if Felix flew down to spend the last week in March with her; and so it might have been in the ordinary way. This year, however, the Grand National was to be run in that particular week, a fact which to Felix's way of thinking made the project clearly unfeasible. He had written to say so, never dreaming for a moment that the excuse could be found inadequate; and, after a silence of three weeks, had been stunned by this long telegram, giving details of horses destroyed in that grueling race over the past twenty years and ending up: "distressed inform you find your whole way going about things in highest degree odd."

Miss Horniman was rich and the only surviving member of the family except for Felix himself. Having already run through a large part of his father's fortune, the young man experienced now and again a twinge of anxiety as to his future. He naturally expected, in the fullness of time, to run through Miss Horniman's wealth as well; and even if, as he frequently reminded himself to hope, this might not be for a long while yet, the thought of it gave him an agreeable sense of security. But once Miss Horniman decided he was odd, anything could happen. She would not, he imagined, be so wicked as to cut him out altogether, but she was fully capable of tying her money up in some eccentric way to prevent his touching the capital. His father had attempted to do the same, and it had cost Felix no end of time and trouble and lawyer's fees to get things straightened out. Where money was concerned, the pair of them had no more sense than children, he reflected gloomily as he strode along, and they apparently believed he could

live on air; they had always been out of touch with
the realities of modern life.

In this dark strain his thoughts ran on when, opposite the Morgan Gallery, he saw a sight that halted
him in his tracks. A youth was leaning against the
stone balustrade, his head buried in his arms and his
whole attitude indicative of final, hopeless despair. He
was groaning a little. Felix could never bear to see
anyone unhappy, man, woman, child or beast, and his
own worries, sharp as they were, immediately left his
head. He silently watched the bowed figure for a
moment or two, and then he went up and spoke to
him.

"Hullo, I say. Anything up? Can I help you?"

Tommy O'Driscoll indeed was undergoing the extremes of misery and humiliation. His instructions
had been to reach the Gallery by eleven o'clock, as the
Bombardier understood that everyone in England
was having a cup of tea at that hour, and there would
be less danger of interference. As soon as Liam also
appeared and took up his position, he was to enter
the Gallery quietly and boldly, locate the picture
from a plan supplied by the Organization, secure it,
walk out unconcernedly with it under his arm and
hand it over to Liam, who was to have a taxi waiting
around the corner. Having telegraphed to "Cartwright" and received his answer, they were to meet
again at an agreed address and proceed with the re-
moval of the picture to Ireland. As the Bombardier
had explained it, the scheme had appeared to be fool-
proof, and yet, for its entire success, it did depend,
quite apart from accidents, on two factors, of which
both were unhappily missing.

First, it was essential that Liam should be there.
But twelve o'clock was striking now, and there was no

sign of him. At home Tommy was never surprised if a man failed to keep an appointment, often indeed was unaware of it, having failed to appear himself; but this old Irish custom seemed inappropriate in circumstances like the present. He knew that Liam had caught the boat, for he had seen him on board drinking with some English strangers in the bar and apparently in the best of spirits. At one point he had raised his glass with the cry, "To the Island of Saints and Scholars, and the shortest way out of it!" and Tommy had much admired the aplomb with which he played his role. But where was he now?

Second, and equally important, Tommy would have to find the courage to enter the Gallery and steal the picture. It had never crossed his mind that there would be any difficulty about this part of it. Since leaving the Bombardier on Sunday afternoon, he had performed the feat in his imagination so often, with such careless grace and valor, that he supposed it would come as second nature. But once he stood in front of the Gallery and looked at the broad stone steps that led up to it, with their crouching stone lions, and at the great doors, and the high, polished windows staring mindlessly at him, he was seized by panic. If he were caught . . . He would be put in prison and he knew what English prisons were. The warders there were the most brutal men alive. They would beat him and torture him to make him confess to crimes he had never committed; they would pin the I.R.A. bombings and shootings on him and keep him in jail for the rest of his life. The letter he had so pleasurably composed to his mother would really have to be posted; and he would never see his frying pan again. At that moment Tommy believed all the stories about the English that he had ever heard, as well as a number he had thought of in the first place himself, and his very bones seemed to melt with terror.

At the sound of Felix's voice he looked up and stared piteously at him. There stood a man of about thirty, short, lithe, alert as a squirrel, and the embodiment of all Tommy disliked and feared: English, beautifully dressed and expensively shod, and with a horrible ease and assurance of manner; and yet with so kind and compassionate a look in his eyes that in spite of himself Tommy answered, "Oh, I'm in trouble, all right."

"Why, you are from Ireland, I do believe!" Felix exclaimed.

Tommy drew himself up at once and inquired stiffly, "Anything strange about that?"

"Strange, indeed! I should think not. My favorite country in the whole world. Look here," he said, laying a hand on Tommy's sleeve, "my Club is just round the corner. Two heads are better than one, even when mine's of the party. We'll have a small drink and go thoroughly into this case of yours together."

"Ah, I could never do that," Tommy began in alarm.

"Nonsense. Up the Irish! Horniman's my name. This way."

It was a characteristic of Tommy O'Driscoll that he invariably responded to friendly behavior. A person had only to smile at him and at once he felt his heart expand and glow. Sometimes this amiable quality would militate against his own interest; at Kitchen Accessories, for example, if ladies were nice to him he would often advise them on no account to buy the company's wares but to go down the road to a rival concern where, he thought, they might be better pleased. The present was no exception. Felix might be English, but there was such a warmth in his manner, he showed himself so anxious to help, that Tommy's defenses were down in no time at all; and very soon, as they sat in the Club's armchairs, he was pouring out the whole story of the legacy and the painting and the Organization. Once he began, the words came with such a rush that he could not have stopped himself if he would.

Felix listened enthralled, and as Tommy finished speaking, threw himself back in his chair with a shout of laughter.

"Oh, you Irish! You devils! There's no one like you," he cried, gazing at the other with intense admiration. "The brains of you, to think out a thing like that! And the pluck, to carry it through! O'Driscoll, I'm proud to know you. Yes, but look here. What's the matter, then? For you were looking the picture of misery when I floated by."

"Because Liam never turned up," Tommy said. "And I'm afraid he's arrested. The Organization warned us of the dangers we ran. I'd a feeling we were being shadowed on the boat. And I can never do it alone."

"Then count me in," said Felix promptly. "What's more, I'll pinch the picture for you. That old bison, Wilberforce! He's a member of this Club, always complaining. There's nothing I'd enjoy so much as popping a hornet in his drawers."

"Ah, but you mustn't! Why should you?" Tommy cried. "Something terrible might happen to you, and I'd be to blame. And it's an Irishman's job."

"Stuff. It's the least I can do. Monstrous, that you weren't given your picture decently years ago. Quick sharp. I'm lunching at one-thirty and mustn't be late; hand over the plan and I'm off."

Felix's whole face was alight with interest and amusement and, as Tommy in spite of himself obeyed, he seized the sketch and pored over it with the air of a commander in the field.

"Right," he said at last with a happy little sigh. "Now you sit here and finish your drink in peace. Don't worry about me. I won't be caught and, anyway, no one would dare come looking in here. Back in ten minutes."

He was out of the room with his springing walk before Tommy had time to reply. The seconds slowly passed, beaten out by an ancient grandfather clock. The patriot's heart beat painfully, too, and he could hardly breathe; and by the time that Felix returned with a canvas under his arm he was almost ready to faint.

"All clear! Child's play. I never met a soul. The staff must be on its annual outing. Now I don't know what you will say to this," Felix remarked, with the wheedling air of a salesman, "but the fact is, those goat pictures are too frightful. Of course, I know all about the artist expressing his vision splendid, but Ireland is a decent agricultural country, and when it comes to goats the people know what's what. So what I've done is to bring you instead—strictly on appro. of course—this rather sweet old party, glug-glugging away at the infuriator." And he proudly displayed a Toulouse-Lautrec, entitled *"La Vieille Ivrogne."*

"Sure, that'll never do!" cried Tommy in horror. "My orders were to bring one of the legacy pictures. The principle is the thing; it doesn't matter at all if the picture is good or bad."

"But from the artistic point of view—" Felix protested.

"Ireland isn't interested in art," Tommy informed

him, in a tone that put art in its place forever. "Ireland wants justice. And I have my orders, which I disregard at my peril."

"Say no more, Brigadier. It was just a notion I took," said Felix, in gay acquiescence; and, tucking the picture under his arm again, he departed to make the exchange.

A number of conflicting emotions filled Tommy's breast as he sat and waited. He admired Felix for his boldness, and envied and disliked him for it at the same time; he was both amused and exasperated by his frivolity; and while he was grateful for his help in Ireland's cause, there was something shocking to his puritanical mind in the fact of its being given. Over all these feelings predominated one of apprehension so cruel as to make him physically weak and helpless. Members of the Club were now entering the great room in twos and threes, and it struck him that they looked curiously and suspiciously in his direction. Presently one of them murmured something to a waiter, who shot a glance at him before murmuring back. The presence of a strange young man with a mop of red curls and dressed in noticeable tweed, who, further, was deadly white in the face and quivering like a hare, might fairly arouse some comment in any London club of conservative tradition; but Tommy did not realize this. Suddenly it flashed across his mind that he was in a trap. All that had been mysterious in the encounter with Felix Horniman became plain: this kind stranger was no friend, but a spy put on him by the British Secret Service, and when he returned it would be with the police. Very likely Liam was a spy as well, and had denounced him; that would explain his nonappearance at the Gallery. His thoughts raced wildly on like an engine out of control until, with a great effort, he pulled himself together and tore out of the building as fast as his legs would carry him.

When Felix came back with the Lafuente y Chaos he was anything but pleased to find his confederate gone.

"Surely, Tasker, Mr. O'Driscoll left a message, didn't he?" he grumbled to the hall porter.

"No, sir. He flashed past me without a word."

"How extremely odd." Felix meditated, frowning, for a few seconds. "Well, put some paper and string round that picture, will you? If Mr. O'Driscoll comes in, you may give it to him."

"Certainly, sir."

"And, Tasker. Better not mention the picture to anyone. It's out of the Morgan Gallery, you see. It belongs to Ireland really, and Mr. O'Driscoll was sent over here by a secret society to take it home."

"Very good, sir."

Felix hurried away to keep his luncheon appointment, still feeling a little ruffled. It's all very well, but I'm a busy man, he thought to himself.

Later in the afternoon, however, he took a rosier view of matters. For one thing, he had enjoyed himself extremely at old Mrs. Windlesham's luncheon party; she always remembered what he liked to eat and drink and took care to invite only handsome young women. And this morning, after all, had been spent in a delightfully unusual way. He had never worked for a secret society before, and he loved anything new. Also, he had felt curiously drawn to Tommy, who reminded him of someone he had known in the past long ago, somebody wistful and appealing who had made an impression at some moment, although he could not for the life of him think who it was.

On reaching his Club again he found with pleasure that the story of the Lafuente y Chaos had already got into the evening papers. There was little as yet but the simple report of the theft and the comments, obviously pruned, of Sir Alvary Wilberforce; and, having ordered tea, he sat down in joyous expectancy to wait for the later editions.

He was greatly astonished, when they came, by the stir his simple action had caused, and his private knowledge of this one affair led him to think that the state of the world in general might not be as black as it was commonly painted. It was, he discovered, the work of the Irish Republican Army, carefully and ruthlessly planned for months before, and most probably the first of a number of attacks on the artistic heritage of the English people. A sawed-off shotgun, recently found in one of the cloakrooms at Euston Station, was thought to have a bearing on the matter. The police were looking for a man with a scarred face and a Cork accent, who, they believed, might help them in their inquiries. A watch was being kept on all the ports. The Irish Embassy had expressed its regret, while drawing attention to the fact that as long as Partition continued in force, such incidents were inevitable.

Editorial comment was no less bewildering. One paper, linking the episode with race-gangs, Teddy boys, erotic dance music and the general depravity of the times resulting from the merciless taxation of the middle classes, resumed its campaign for the re-introduction of flogging with fresh spirit. Another, successfully sued by Sir Alvary twenty-five years ago, drew

a horrifying picture of the national collections slowly
dwindling away while their appointed guardians, paid
from the public money, lolled about in cushioned
ease. Readers of *The London Post,* whose motto of
"Floreat Britannia" suggested a different approach,
were surprised to find the raiders warmly congratulated on their courage and patriotic feeling; they
were not to know that the leader-writer had fallen ill
and that his deputy, a Mr. Kevin O'Toole, had been
hastily fetched from the local tavern to take his place.
A surprise of a different kind was the reticence of Mr.
Evelyn Burbage. Dublin had in fact telephoned to
him for an informed English opinion, but, deep in a
closely reasoned study of the Opium War, he had
merely replied, "Oh, leave me alone, will you?"

Felix looked up to find the porter standing beside
him, staring at the wall above his head, like the sound
ex-Guardsman he was, and coughing.

"Speak, Tasker, good soul," he prayed him.

"The party never called back for his property, sir,"
Tasker informed him, staring upwards with appalled
eyes. "And Sir Alvary is inside, sir. In a fearful
taking."

"Aha. Aha."

"There's the Club to be studied, sir, when all is
said and done," propounded Tasker in an expiring
voice.

"Relax, faithful guardian of us all; the matter re-
ceives attention." And, leaving the porter weary and
limp from the effort of taking a liberty, Felix went
to the telephone happy as a boy planning a raid on an
orchard, to put in a call to an old and trusted friend.

"Badger, dear thing," he said when a creaking
rumble was heard at the end of the wire, "how is that
old bus of yours? Will she stay in the air?"

"Course she will, Felix. What silly questions you ask. She was never better in her life."

"Then we fly to Ireland directly."

"Before dinner?" came in shocked tones.

"Afraid so. There is not a moment to lose."

"What have you been up to now, Felix?"

Felix briefly explained the matter, emphasizing the scruples of the porter, a man of whom his friend the Badger was extremely fond; but when he had finished speaking there was a long silence.

"Are you there?"

"Course I'm there, Felix, where else should I be? I was only thinking. I don't much like the sound of it."

"Come, come! Yoicks tally-ho! Aren't you a sportsman nowadays?"

"I am a sportsman, I hope," responded the Badger gravely. "But I am also a Justice of the Peace. And I made a resolve, after the last time, not to be out with you again without consulting the Clerk beforehand. The Clerk had something to say about that other business. He thinks a Justice of the Peace ought to be careful."

"Well, ring him up now and see what he says."

"He takes his sister to the moving pictures on Tuesday," said the Badger in a peevish tone. "He will not be at home before ten."

"Too late. Wilberforce is baying like a bloodhound in the billiard room. Of course, if you are going to let me down . . ." Felix faltered.

"Oh, I'll come, if you're going to cry," the Badger said testily. "I was only thinking, I don't much like the sound of it."

Major Henry Cattermole, M.C., D.S.O., Justice of the Peace and Master of Foxhounds, known to his friends as the Badger, kept his airplane at an aviation club on the edge of London. A man whose mental processes were of the leisurely kind, he loved physical speed above all else, and his small, old-fashioned machine was the apple of his eye. He needed little coaxing to take to the air with her on whatever pretext; and by the time Felix arrived with the picture and his bag he was already in flying kit and surveying her with fond delight.

"Asking for trouble," he said complacently. "Dublin knows we're coming, but it'll be a darkish landing. Guesswork, really. I often think of getting some instruments."

The flight proceeded smoothly and without incident, except that about halfway across the Irish Channel the plane suddenly went into a steep nose dive, as if determined to plunge into the water.

"Badger, dear soul."

"Sorry," the pilot roared back, laughing, as he pulled her out of it. "I was just thinking. Often go into a dive when I'm thinking."

"What were you thinking about?"

"The Customs. What will you say?"

"Nothing."

"Can't hear."

"Nothing!"

"Oh."

The Customs officer at Dublin received them with all the warmth and courtesy of his race, but, as was his right, he did go into the matter of the painting. He examined it carefully, upside down and sideways, with pursed lips and a bewildered look on his face, while Felix fidgeted a little and the Badger gazed stolidly in front of him.

"There's supposed to be a duty on this class of

article now," the officer said. "Would it be an heir-loom, sir?"

"No."

The man resumed his study of the picture, when all at once he stiffened and his whole demeanor under-went a sudden change. Seizing the newspaper with which the careful Tasker had lined the package, he waved it in front of their eyes and said severely, "You'll have to leave that here. The *News of the World* is not allowed into Ireland."

"I'm very sorry, I didn't know."

"Then you ought to know."

"But what do you all read on Sunday morning?" the Badger inquired in honest amazement.

The man ignored the question, and having re-placed the brown paper and string around the canvas, gave it back and motioned them on. Then he tripped away to his own quarters at speed with the confiscated print.

"Now for a cab. It's barely ten," Felix said cheer-fully. "Well, that's that, Badger old scout, thanks to you. Extraordinary how simple life is, if you go about things in a simple way. Let's go to the Club and have some of their glorious pie."

The suggestion appealed to the Badger immensely. At the Club, however, there was a great surprise in store, and one not at all to their liking. As they passed the pigeonholes for members' letters and belongings they noted, crammed into the one marked B, a velvet tea cozy, a flute, an eighteenth-century pistol and a bundle of rhubarb. On the floor beneath were two croquet sticks, a Persian saddlebag, a sketching easel, a sack of potatoes, a kettledrum and a Bunsen burner.

"Well, Brian, are we holding our rummage sale this evening, or what?" Felix asked.

The old man shook his head with a mournful smile. "They're Mrs. Barry's personal property, sir, God help us!"

"And who, pray, is Mrs. Barry?"

"She is a member of this Club, sir."

Neither Felix nor the Badger could altogether believe his ears.

"Surely you are joking," Felix began nervously. "How could a lady be a member of this Club?"

"It's a sign of the times, sir," Brian told him in a lugubrious voice. "We couldn't keep going without them. Kildare Street's got them as well. The United Services has them under consideration. God be with the days when the British were here! I've seen plenty of change, and all for the worse, but I never imagined I'd live to see this." He heaved a sigh. "Not that Mrs. Barry isn't a lovely lady," he added, "but it's like having a typhoon in the building. We were never used to it."

"Well, mind this parcel for me, will you?" said Felix dully.

The two men went in silence to the Buttery, where they ordered smoked salmon, the Club's cold pie, Stilton cheese and pints of ale in a vain attempt to revive their spirits. They were so stunned by the news they had just received that they hardly knew what they ate, and neither had any inclination to talk; they munched away in silence, with dark forebodings, visions of a ruined world, passing through their minds.

"What shall you do about the picture?" the Badger asked presently, with a conscious effort.

"Eh? Oh, that. I must try and find the young man, I suppose. Or something."

There was another gloomy silence.

"Why not just hand it over yourself?" then proceeded the Badger without interest.

"What's that? Oh, come now," said Felix, rousing himself a little. "We were mean enough, I fancy, in stealing their picture from them. We really can't pinch the credit of bringing it back."

The Badger grunted.

In this manner the bequest of Afrodisio Lafuente y Chaos came to Ireland. Meanwhile, the foreign correspondents in London were filing their copy, and the exploit of the I.R.A., gallant or outrageous, was about to reach the world at large. It was to penetrate, in time, to the remote village of Torremolinos, where it gave rise to a typically uncharitable and uncalled-for observation on the part of Miss Horniman. Pausing in the act of rescuing hapless jellyfish, cast up on the beach by the insensate cruelty of the Spanish tide, she remarked, "That is the kind of extremely odd behavior I should expect of my nephew Felix."

five

"Go on," said Mrs. Barry. "Tell me some more."

"There is no more to tell," Tommy replied, folding his arms.

He had not yet returned to business, as his friend Dr. McGrath had certified that it would be a week at least before he was fit to do so. With a pleasant sense of freedom he sat on an upturned box in the garden and watched his Landlord at work. She was clearing a patch of ground in which she proposed, experimentally, to plant a mango tree, for it was her belief that the soil of her garden would grow anything, given a chance.

"But what happened then? It was just getting interesting," she said, fishing a broken teapot out of the ground and examining it critically before she threw it away. "After you got the picture, what did you do?"

"I handed it over to my lieutenant, who was waiting in a taxi," he told her casually. He hesitated for a moment, aware that modesty becomes the hero; but then his need for communication got the better of him as usual, and he swept on: "The hue and cry had already begun. Oh, it was desperate! I had to knock one of the fellows senseless before I could get away."

"You did?" asked Mrs. Barry, looking at him intently.

"I did. And that is the end of my story."

"And a very good story too. How would it be," Mrs. Barry inquired with a motherly air, "if you told it to the Marines as well?"

"Do you imply," Tommy cried, flushing scarlet, "that I am not speaking the truth?"

He was cut to the heart by her lack of confidence. For some reason that he had never quite fathomed, he was most anxious to have her good opinion; and with the glorious success of the raid in London it had seemed to him at last that this must be assured. And he was not only hurt, but angry and disappointed as well. She was displaying a mean, suspicious side to her nature that he would never have thought existed. He had told her beforehand that he was about to leave England on dangerous business, and now the fame of it was ringing round the world. But for him none of it would have happened; and, instead of giving him the ungrudging admiration he felt was his due, she was actually calling him a liar. Somehow or other it took the cream off the whole affair for him, although he told himself that this was absurd.

"Nothing of the kind!" she said merrily. "I only thought the Marines would enjoy it too."

He lapsed into silence, moodily biting a finger.

"And I wouldn't want to believe it, either," she added. "A most disgraceful affair! Bloody Sinn Feiners!" At the idea of conduct so entirely outrageous, she gave one of her joyous shouts of laughter.

A bent figure, whose matted hair was crowned with the brim of an old straw hat, shambled out of the house with the air of expecting a missile. It was Peadar, the right-hand man, whose manifold duties included that of butler.

"There's one inside now, ma'am, that has urgent business with yourself," he began warily.

"I don't see anyone except by appointment. You know that," Mrs. Barry replied, plunging her fork into the ground. "Tell him to ring me up."

"The gentleman was telephoning the whole of yesterday, ma'am, he told me," Peadar pleaded.

"So that's what it was! I thought it would never stop," cried his employer indignantly. "And what does he want? Did he say who he was?"

"He did not, ma'am. He said only he must see you at once. He's a grand-looking young fellow, a lord, it wouldn't surprise me."

"Indeed," said Mrs. Barry, brightening a little. "Well, what keeps you standing there? Why don't you show him out?" Why do I pay that blockhead? she ruminated, her eyes fixed malevolently on Peadar's sad, retreating back.

As Felix came into the garden, only the perfect manners that had been beaten into him in the nursery prevented the wrath that seethed in his bosom from finding expression. It was not enough that the Royal Hibernian was ruined forever by the admission of lady members, nor that one of these same ladies should clutter the venerable place with objects better suited, he told himself furiously, to the nest of a magpie, but this lady herself must needs make off, along with her own indescribable gear, with a picture belonging to him, or rather to the Irish people. She was no better than a plague of locusts; such had been

Brian's opinion when, after searching high and low for the missing canvas, he had at last divined the truth. Not only that, but Felix had been kept running to the telephone all the next day in the attempt to get hold of her, when he might have been enjoying himself with his friends; and this morning he had been obliged to hire a car and drive to her house, when he ought to have been at a point-to-point in Clonmel. That sort of woman could ruin a man's whole life, he reflected.

"Do forgive this horrid intrusion," he began with his sweetest air. "My name is Horniman. Well, I'm blest!"

The ejaculation related, of course, to Tommy O'Driscoll, who was staring at him with his mouth open.

"So that's it! You're here! And is she in it too?" he exclaimed, forgetting himself in his excitement.

"If you mean the Cat's Mother, she probably is," Mrs. Barry dryly observed.

"Oh, I do beg your pardon! How frightfully rude," Felix said with remorse. "But, you see, it was the shock of seeing O'Driscoll here when I thought the rest of my life would be spent in looking for him. What on earth happened to you?" he asked querulously. "We brought the picture over by plane. It was like the best sort of melodrama, expect that nobody seemed to care. The wicked flee when none pursueth, and all that. I was racking my brains about what to do next. Advertising for you seemed indiscreet. Have you seen the papers? Ports watched! Suspects questioned! Sir Alvary indisposed! You're a national hero."

"Ah, now, now," said Tommy, his eyes modestly cast on the ground.

Mrs. Barry rose majestically from the sack on which she was crouching, to her full height of five foot two, dusting her small, grubby hands as she did so.

"You don't mean to say," she asked, "that what Mr. O'Driscoll has been telling me about his adventures in London was the truth?"

"Why, of course it was," Felix said cheerfully. "It's all in the newspapers."

"I do not read the newspapers," Mrs. Barry informed him. She surveyed her tenant in silence for a while, and then an alarming change took place in her appearance. A reddening of the face and neck, as of a turkey cock in full pride, was accompanied by convulsive tremors through the whole little frame; the eyes were tightly shut and the hands moved to and fro in the air as if seeking a support. Unfamiliar with her procedures, Felix was on the point of springing forward to loosen something when the climax came and passed; together with a gradual return to normal color, there was a shattering burst of sound. Mrs. Barry was amused, and was signifying as much in the whole-hearted manner of the Anglo-Irish gentry.

It was some little time before anyone could be heard speak, but when at last there came a lull, Felix availed himself of it to say, "The only thing is, I think you have got the picture here. You must have taken it from the Royal Hibernian yesterday morning, with the rest of your property."

The Landlord trumpeted with new fury. "The Royal Hibernian," she crowed. "And now in my attic!" With a prodigious effort, she pulled herself together. "You are not to suppose," she said severely, with a tear of merriment running down her cheek, "that I approve of this. If I'd known you were that sort of fellow, Tommy, you should never have had my flat. There were never Sinn Feiners in the house before.

"I'm very proud of you," she added incoherently. Her face suddenly crumpled as if she were going to cry. "This deserves a drink," she said in a strangled voice. "Get out the chairs, Tommy, till I fetch one."

Tommy obediently collected the three wooden boxes that went by this name, while Mrs. Barry tore into the house.

"Well, well, well!" said Felix, seating himself gingerly while the fresh April breezes nipped his ears. "Well, well, well, well, well!" It was all he could think of to say. "Well, well," he added for greater emphasis.

"It was the Will of God," said Tommy, as one who enjoyed that Being's confidence.

"But where on earth were you, active soul? I might never have found you."

"I went for a taxi, to have it waiting for you," Tommy informed him readily, "and, unaccustomed to the roar of London traffic, I was knocked down by one. When next I opened my eyes I was lying on a stretcher in the casualty hall of a great hospital, and a girl in a white uniform was bending over me. But don't let's talk about me," he said, shrugging the episode off. "You are much more interesting. How in the Name of God did you go walking in and out of that Gallery with their pictures under your arm?"

Felix laughed delightedly. "That's the best part of it," he cried, "and I never knew it till last night. Old Badger—that's the man who flew me over—rang up from London to tell me. There wasn't a living soul about in the Gallery when I went in; the reason being, that old dunce Wilberforce had been tipped off by anonymous letter that a raid was coming, and had

collected all the attendants together for a little talk
on security."

"An anonymous letter!" stammered Tommy, turning pale. "Who will have written that?"

"Well, he didn't say, you know."

"But only the Bombardier and Liam knew anything about it! It must have been Liam. The dirty
hound! Who knows what mightn't have happened to
me?" exclaimed Tommy in retrospective panic.

"And something did happen to you, poor fellow.
How do you feel now, after your accident?"

"What accident was that?" asked Tommy vaguely.
His mind was full of Liam's treachery, and in any
case he tended to live in the present.

"Why, when the cab knocked you down."

"Ah, for God's sake!" Pedantic fellows the English,
he thought.

Felix was much impressed by his stoicism and did
not labor the point, as a new and important idea had
occurred to him. "What about this lady here?" he
asked. "Is she on our side or not?"

The object of his inquiry herself would have been
puzzled to find a reply. She had gone into the house
with every intention of preparing drink to celebrate
the occasion. She had an ineradicable Edwardian
fondness for what she called a "jape," and Tommy's
exploit appealed to her as a jape of the finest quality.
It surpassed by far any of the notable japes that had
come her way in the past, which, if deeply satisfying,
had been simple and as a rule connected with
chamber pots. Not that she had been idle in the field
herself. Only a month or two since she had called on
some pompous neighbors under an assumed name,
her head swathed in a beekeeper's veil, her diction
obscured by a set of teeth cut from the peel of an

orange, a disguise she had supposed from the bewildered faces of her hosts to have been impenetrable.
With the whole of one side of her rich nature she
responded to this new, enchanting prank; shaking all
over with mirth, she got as far as placing a tooth mug,
a chipped Coronation beaker and a small flower vase
on the tray, and a retort of her own elderberry wine
on the stove to warm.

Then her eye fell on a portrait of George V dressed
in nautical attire, which set up a new train of ideas
altogether. She thought of her friends burned out of
ancestral halls by the likes of Tommy. She considered
the horrors of the present regime, where you never
knew what extraordinary person might not be beside
you at dinner. Crossly, she told herself she was no
better than a *sansculotte,* and she whipped the elderberry wine off the stove again. Next, she wondered
if this young Horniman was anything to that Lucius
Horniman with whom as a girl she had danced in
Delhi. There was something about those gay brown
eyes . . . but, if so, he was no better than a *sansculotte.* From there the natural thing was to picture
Captain Horniman's face if he could see what his
young relation was up to; and the inevitable consequence of that was another fit of trumpeting. The
poor woman hardly knew whether she was on her
head or her heels. What she needed to steady her was
a basis for reaction: an Englishman there to assail
Tommy, when she would have hotly defended him,
Sinn Fein and the Republic, or a pack of Sinn Feiners
to applaud, when she would have turned them all out
of the house. In the absence of any such clarifying
agent, she was lost, and stood there helplessly moving
the wine on and off the stove in accordance with her
conflicting impulses.

"She's a great old girl," Tommy replied contentedly. When she had said she was proud of him, it was as if the whole of his life had burst into flower.

"But is she on our side, dear thing?"

"She's not, of course," Tommy said with fondness. "How could she be?"

"Hoo hoo hoo!" came from the interior of the house.

"She seems to be taking it very well, then."

"Ah, she would."

"I don't want to be a bore," Felix persisted, "but it looks as if there will be an almighty row over this. You may have to lie low. Can you trust her?"

"I should think I can," Tommy said indignantly.

"How do you know?"

Felix might as well have asked how Tommy knew the sun would rise on the following morning; it was one of those things that no one goes into. "I do know; that's all," was the reply. "She's not one of us." The words were not, he thought at once, happily chosen; but they expressed his meaning.

"What is she, then?"

"She's the ascendency," Tommy informed him.

"What on earth may that be?"

The young patriot heaved a weary sigh. Such ignorance on the part of a supposedly educated man was wearing his patience down. "The ascendency," he said, with the artificial kindliness of a goaded schoolmaster, "is the class of imported persons who joined with the English in enslaving our country for hundreds of years, destroying its native Gaelic culture and driving its best sons forth to a precarious existence in foreign lands."

"And you really trust her, after she did all that?"

"Didn't you hear me say so?" demanded the other crustily.

Felix decided to drop the matter, as just a little beyond him; and in any case the Landlord now rejoined them, carrying a tray in her hands.

"You boys are in luck, I may tell you," she said. "You nearly didn't get this." And filling each of the receptacles with the hot, amazingly blue liquid, she took an appreciative sip from the flower vase.

Mrs. Barry was a lady who did nothing by halves. She had decided that the occasion was to be festive after all, a decision toward which an honest pride in her elderberry wine and a generous desire to share it with others had considerably helped her; and since it was so, no further chiding passed her lips. The violent start that Felix gave as he swallowed a mouthful of the brew gratified her immensely, and she spared no pains to make the party an agreeable one. She lauded the young men for their pluck, scolded them for not drinking fast enough and promised them it was the jolliest day she had known for months.

"The only things is, the picture is a fright," Felix said presently. "It's no more like goats than I am."

"Is it, indeed! Wait till I see," and she went bounding along the path to the house.

There was no difficulty in finding the parcel, which, as Brian had surmised, she had swept in with the rest of her property and deposited in the one pile. It took her longer to unwrap it, as she could not see what she was doing for laughter. When at last she succeeded, however, her mood underwent one of its abrupt, unpredictable changes. The picture was not like goats or anything else, but was simply a mad riot of crimson, yellow and rose, the color having apparently been hurled at the canvas from some little distance away. The subject could as well have been Sunrise at Simla, or Fried Egg with Tomato, she thought; indeed, half a dozen titles of equal relevance occurred to her. The very signature of the artist in the bottom right-hand corner looked like nothing so much as a roll of barbed wire.

Mrs. Barry contemplated the picture with a steadily rising indignation. She was herself an artist of a different school: her horses were real horses, her flowers stood in their vase indeed, and there was a notable verisimilitude about her dead pheasants and bunches of grapes. Added to this, she had a deep affection for goats, as for all of the animal world, and she had a sense of looking on while friends of hers were cruelly defamed. Memories of dear, loyal goats she had known came flocking into her mind, reviving her own loyal sentiments and fanning her mistrust of the Irish Republic.

"Goats indeed!" she barked.

For a while longer she stood and glowered at the canvas. She had a very good mind to burn it immediately. All her pleasure in Tommy's magnificent jape was gone. Then suddenly, in a flash, there came to her inspiration, a notion of such pure, intense beauty that the light of divilment, never extinguished for long, burned in her eye like a clear little beacon. An expression almost of awe came over her face. A few moments later the young men shivering on their boxes in the garden heard sounds suggestive now of a hunting horn of uncommon power, now of a herd of elephants in headlong, panic flight. For all the warring conceptions that fretted her soul the Landlord had found the perfect synthesis.

SIX

Uncertainty as to the picture's whereabouts had prevented Tommy from communicating with his Chief until now. It was one thing to glide over that part of the story as he told it to Mrs. Barry; but his report to the Organization would require a more factual approach. The message he sent, through the roundabout channels agreed on, left nothing to be desired in this respect, stating simply that the mission had been completed, that he had been obliged through unforeseen circumstances to carry it out alone and that he awaited further instructions. To his utter amazement, there was no reply at all. Early each morning he ran downstairs, all day long at the shop he was in a fever of impatience to get home, to see if anything in the Bombardier's distinguished writing, with its huge square letters, its uncrossed t's and undotted i's, had come by the post; but one day followed another and the great man's silence was unbroken. The situation began to affect his nerves.

"Thank goodness you're here," he exclaimed one evening to Felix. "It's a terrible responsibility for one man to take. Oh, why doesn't he write to me?"

In consequence of his proving to be in fact the nephew of the late Colonel Lucius Horniman, Felix had been requisitioned by Mrs. Barry. She simply would not hear of his going away. To begin with he put up a token resistance, as the rigors of Irish country houses were foreign to his way of life. But there was nothing of much importance in London at the moment, he was curious to see the end of Tommy's adventure, he was enchanted by the Landlord herself, and he therefore capitulated. He bought any number of pajamas, ties and shirts, sent funny post cards to his friends, hired a Daimler and settled down to await developments.

"It's certainly very odd of him not to," he now remarked.

"Odd!" said Tommy, firing up. He was in a difficult mood these days. "There's nothing odd about the Bombardier."

"Hm."

"You think everyone's odd who is not like yourself."

Felix thought precisely that, but was too polite to insist on it. "Why does he call himself the Bombardier?" he asked, hoping to steer the conversation into safer waters.

"How do I know? Why should he not? The questions you ask!"

"I tell you what," Felix said briskly. "Our charming hostess is out on safari this evening. How would it be if I drove you to town for a spot of dinner?"

"You think a spot of dinner's the solution to everything."

"So it is," replied the incorrigible materialist. "Are you coming?"

"Oh, all right."

To the world at large, meanwhile, the affair of the Morgan Gallery raid remained unclear. The Irish Government refused to commit itself. No one knew where the picture was, it said, and there was as yet no evidence to show that the I.R.A. were really involved. It would be time enough to consider the matter when such evidence should be made available. This cautious approach was not shared by the public, which was talking its head off in the wildest manner and enjoying itself immensely. It was a put-up job on the part of Sir Alvary Wilberforce, or even the English Prime Minister, to discredit Ireland. It was Roger Casement all over again, said the partisans of this view. Others, again, were in a position to reveal that it was the I.R.A. all the time, as they knew a man who had a brother in that glorious body. It was about time the country grew up, said some; others repined that no blood had been shed. The one thing that united the different schools of thought was a profound satisfaction at Ireland's reaching the head-lines again, the limited amount of space devoted by the Press of the world, as a rule, to Irish affairs being a regular source of grief and surprise.

After careful thought, Tacky called an extraordinary meeting of his committee. The purpose of it was to discuss what their attitude should be if the I.R.A. were to offer the Lafuente to the Irish Prado; or so he said in the convening notices. He did not believe for a moment that the I.R.A. were concerned in the matter, nor had the Irish Prado been mentioned by anyone as a possible beneficiary, but he was a man who looked ahead, as well as around and up and down. To his great relief, Miss Scully was absent. She was busy at home, marking passages in a recent novel to be sent with a strong letter to the Censorship Board, a duty she estimated to take precedence over any other. With Miss Scully away, Lady Twomey was much more amenable, while the men were no trouble at all. In less than seven minutes, agreement was reached that on the whole their best plan was simply to wait and see what happened.

Tacky had expected no less. "It's a privilege to sit on a Cŏmmĭttēē like this one!" he declared, smiling broadly and rubbing his hands.

As they had time to spare, he went on to discuss a question—of no great importance, he emphasized, and very much of the future; but it was well to be prepared, wasn't that right? Visitors to the Irish Prado might want to take away some little memento of the pictures they had enjoyed. It would keep the experience fresh in their minds, and bring money to the Institution. He thought that colored post cards would serve the purpose, something like the grand series they were putting out now for Killarney and places. If the Committee wished it, he could go into the matter further.

Again, the Committee was disposed to be helpful.

"It's a great idea," Mr. MacMahon said thoughtfully. "But the cards would have to be good ones. They would get posted abroad."

Mr. Connolly thought they ought to be like the ones you got in Paris, with things stuck on them.

"In the case of contemporary pictures, I suppose the artist would get a royalty?" Seumas Cullen inquired.

"You would, of course," the Chairman promised.

"Have we the resources over here?" asked Lady Twomey. "I'm in favor, if so."

"Ah, we have. I've looked into that," Tacky assured her. "The Brian Boru Press has a new department for color blocks and processes that's the better of any in London. And I'm not saying that because I'm Managing Director. We've a man now who's a genius. Everyone's mad to get him. Oh, I agree entirely, it's not a job we'd want to put in just anyone's hands. In fact," he exclaimed, as a thought suddenly came to him, "this Committee, with the grand sense of responsibility it has, might wish to instruct me to give the sole concession to the Brian Boru, the way we could always depend on the quality."

This proposal having been received with acclamation, Tacky undertook to draft a letter, from the Chairman of the Committee to the Managing Director of the Brian Boru Press, along the desired lines. With a sense of achievement, the Committee dispersed. Easter Sunday was four days ahead, and Lady Twomey therefore hurried off to buy a hat she had long coveted in Switzer's. Seumas Cullen went home to write an anonymous letter to a critic. Mr. Connolly dropped into a cinema, where he was soon fast asleep. Finding himself with twenty minutes to spare, Mr. MacMahon went to Confession. Alone in his office, Tacky cogitated.

Another step forward was the positive emerging of Mr. Seán O'Hara as a candidate for the Directorship. A cool April night, spent half in the open air and half in the St. Vincent de Paul refuge for destitute men, whither he had been escorted by a kindly Guard, had persuaded him that something was to be said for an assured position. He continued vehemently to assert that he would ask for nothing, that the job must be pressed on him before he would take it; but he did go so far as to address a formal application to An Taoiseach.

"What's this, the fellow's name is?" he asked, leaning his elbows on the bar and staring in a baffled kind of way at his butty Nolan.

"Ah, don't bother with it; put 'Dear Mr. Prime Minister,'" his political adviser told him.

"And his mother was a barefoot girl from Mayo!"

"Don't mind his mother now," Michael implored him. "You won't get far in Ireland if you worry about mothers. And, anyhow, that's just what the other crowd say about it."

"And it's what I say about it," Seán stated belligerently. "And it's what I say again about it. Anyone here feel disposed," he inquired, with a baleful glare round the room, "to try and stop me saying it again?"

As the pair of them were alone in the bar, he was not taken up; and at last, with Michael's help, the letter was finished. Written on a leaf torn from a notebook, its envelope ringed with the marks of a wet tumbler, it did much to strengthen the opinion of those who saw it that something would have to be done for poor O'Hara.

Seán's entry into the lists came at an inopportune moment for Mr. O'Farrell. When the news of it reached him, he had been on the verge of becoming, as he put it, *souffrant.* Dr. Horst von Gudenus, an eminent German art historian and the Director of a Gallery in Düsseldorf, was expected to arrive in Dublin soon; and following his usual practice, Mr. O'Farrell had determined to be indisposed. He shrank from the round of festivities which visits of this kind would entail; he blushed, he would always say, for his countrymen, for their manners, provincialism, ignorance; their mispronunciation of the names of the Masters, he averred, made him shudder. The whole affair would be merely the pretext for a hooley—as he believed it was called. He would now have to postpone his attack, of gout or asthma, while he dealt with the new situation; but, in perfect command of himself as ever, he betrayed no annoyance at all.

"How I can have the temerity"—he smiled—"to continue in the running I do not know. I simply am not qualified. All I can offer is a certain experience, a flair perhaps, even it may be a little knowledge and taste. But what of that? No one has ever picked me out of a gutter. I have never depended, for my sustenance, on the kindness of rich ladies. No one, as far as I know, exclaims at the sound of my name, 'Ah, sure, God help him!' My confidence is appalling."

He next dropped a line to the Bishop of Galway, and having carefully brushed his broad-brimmed hat, set out on a round of calls.

It was perhaps in keeping with the strange destiny of the Irish Prado that, at the very time when Tacky was sparing no effort to lay the foundations of its success, and when battle for the Directorship had been finally joined, extraneous events should occur to push it further still into the mists of the future. First, the men at work on the building itself went on strike. It was not from dissatisfaction with their wages or conditions, or indeed from any usual cause of labor dispute, but from something much more fundamental. A few days previously County Kerry had met County Cork in a hurling match, a fast-moving game which resulted in several broken heads and two hospital cases, one of them grave; and but for the fact that the referee was a parish priest, it must be feared that there would have been bad language as well. One of the builders, from Cork, had passed remarks on the affair which were unacceptable to another, from Kerry. Words were exchanged, and then blows, and then everyone else started passionately taking sides, until at last the foreman decided the only practical course was to declare a strike until tempers should cool. The strike was at once repudiated by the union, which, newly affiliated to one in England, was at pains to appear correct; but the foreman, himself an amateur hurler of standing, enjoyed great prestige among the men and his ruling was loyally obeyed by all.

"I'm not sure about the legality," he observed, "but I know the boys."

Once again, then, the great enterprise was checked and the skeleton building stood deserted and forlorn to the weather, its rudimentary walls embellished now with the slogans "Up Cork!" and "Up Kerry!" in huge black letters.

Again, thinking men and women could sense a danger to it in the Budget, which was announced at about this time. The piteous appeal in the Minister's voice as he urged all classes of the community to break with the habits of a lifetime and to make their income tax returns in full was an indication of how things stood. The Minister went so far as to quote the Gospel on the duty of rendering unto Caesar those things that were his: a plain reference to a recent ecclesiastical sanction of the normal practice on the grounds that, since everyone followed it, not to do so would be merely unfair to oneself and eccentric. He further clapped new taxes on petrol, matches, liquor, tobacco and foreign newspapers, doubled the levy on all imported goods and stated that the Government subsidies for boots, eggs and windowpanes in the Gaeltacht would have to be withdrawn. The last item did not greatly distress the natives of these regions, as they were nearly all at work in England, but it drew an indignant protest from a Scottish admiral, spending his retirement in Connemara. As a whole, the speech found little favor with the public, which decided once again that the country was going to the dogs, and that the Minister himself had a nerve all the same.

"Did you see the crack the fellow made about Caesar and income tax?"

"Oh, desperate."

"And the bold way he came out with it! I'd say he was anti-clerical."

A rumor came to Tacky's ears that caused him to draw his bushy brows together and to sit for a whole half-hour in the contemplative attitude of Rodin's *"Penseur,"* breathing heavily. Then he reached for the telephone and rang up the Prime Minister.

"A fine Budget!" he said with admiration. "Masterly, Tim! Thanks be to God it's you that's in and not a certain other crowd."

"Thanks, Tacky. We'll do our best, depend on it."

"Sure, there's been no one like you in politics since Grattan himself!"

"Ah, g'wan out of it! What can I do for you?"

"There's no truth in a story going round just now, I suppose?"

"Which one would that be, Tacky?"

"Well, a little bird did whisper to me you boys were packing up. And that when a certain crowd came back, they'd discontinue the Prado idea and go on with the building for a lunatic asylum."

The Prime Minister laughed heartily. "It'll be my opposite number who thought of that," he said. "Don't worry, we're sticking. Mind you, the over-crowding in the asylums is bad enough. But the Prado comes first."

"That's the statesman's point of view I'd expect of yourself," Tacky informed him with real grati-tude. "I only asked because our plans for the Prado are long-term ones, and if the building were to go for another purpose, they'd need careful reconsidera-tion." And he rang off in high feather.

An Taoiseach might laugh, but in releasing this canard, the Opposition had acted with its customary shrewdness. Numerous and extensive as they were, the asylums of Ireland had each its waiting list, and it was an open secret that in consequence the medi-cal profession no longer issued certificates in all the cases that called for them. Neither of the chief politi-cal parties was to blame for this state of affairs. It arose simply from the fact that there were more lunatics about than formerly, and had been de-scribed, in a thoughtful leading article on the subject, as the Growing Pains of a Young State. By their base fabrication, the Sons of Erin succeeded first in focus-ing public attention on the matter and then, when An Taoiseach denied the story, in causing him to appear as frivolous and unfeeling. He was a man who put the claims of art, much of it probably foreign, before those of the Irish lunatic, and his prestige waned alarmingly.

The Budget gave rise to one of the stormiest de-bates in the history of the Republic, followed by a pitched battle between individuals in the lobby—

and that on a day when a delegation from Ghana was present, to study Christian democracy at work! What with all these misfortunes, and the economic plight of the country, and the strike at the Prado, the Irishmen All Party began to feel their situation precarious. Energetic, even radical measures were needed if their enemies were to be confounded and their supporters rallied; and it was thought the best plan would be, for a start, if a new postage stamp could be issued. The design approved after long consultation was remarkably fine, showing Hibernia in muslin draperies tipping out a cornucopia symbolical of cultural riches; it was issued in green, lilac and tan at twopence, threepence and fivepence respectively, and in azure at one-and-three for air-mailing to the United States.

seven

The anxiety and suspense created in Tommy's mind by the extraordinary behavior of his Chief were hard to bear, and as time went on they were complicated by feelings of another sort. However selfless the spirit in which he had undertaken the task laid upon him, he was after all only human. It seemed right, now that the perils were over and victory achieved, that there should be some little recognition of the part he had played in it all. By now he ought to have been a national figure, taking his place as of right among the best of the land. Instead of this, he was catching the bus to work every day and selling pots and pans, was scolded by his employer and laughed at by the typist, like any nonentity.

"I did it for the country, not for myself," he remarked to Felix, "but I do think the country should know."

Felix agreed absolutely.

One morning the young patriot received a letter which struck him as the most shameless ever to be written, and all but destroyed his faith in mankind. It began: "A Chara! So you pulled it off!" and came from Liam Mac Lamh in England. The wretch did not even congratulate him, but went straight on to describe his new, exciting life. He had almost immediately found a place in an advertising agency at twelve pounds a week, and his hopes of advancement were high. The landlady of his delightful lodgings in Hampstead treated him like a son. Why should not Tommy come over at once and try his luck as well, instead of moldering away in Ireland? The cynicism of such a proposal was revolting enough to Tommy's mind, but it was the PS.—"To think I owe it all to the Bombardier!"—that struck him as the last depth of infamy. Having telephoned to the shop to say he was indisposed, he devoted the rest of the day to an answer that should bring the traitor to a decent sense of shame. A few days later a post card of the Queen Trooping the Color arrived, with the simple message: "Come off it, governor! Billy Hand." Tommy saw that the man was lost.

As had become his practice in moments of doubt, he ran to Felix, and showed him the deplorable correspondence from his erstwhile comrade in arms. Felix read it gravely through without making a comment, except to ask, "Why does he sign himself Hand if his name is Mac Lamh?"

"Hand in the Anglicized form of it, of course," Tommy informed him. "That shows you how low he has sunk. A man with a good Irish name!"

"A Hand is a Mac Lamh is a Hand," Felix observed, "and all of doubtful sweetness."

"There's no need to pass any remarks, then!" Tommy flared up, sensing an affront in any allusion that escaped him. "And ignorance is nothing to be proud of."

"There, there," Felix soothed him. "I'm bitterly ashamed of my ignorance, really. Just trying to put a good face on it, you know. Well, so much for the brave Billy. Where do you go from here?"

Tommy controlled the irritation that Saxon levity always aroused in him, and explained the position as he now saw it. The Bombardier's silence was incomprehensible, but it was a fact; it was likewise a fact that Liam's true nature was now laid bare. That the picture was still in Mrs. Barry's attic was another fact, and a fourth was that this picture was the rightful possession of Ireland. After earnest consideration, he had decided the time had come to intervene.

Felix, as always, gave him every support. "That's the stuff, dear thing!" he cried joyously. "You can't wait forever, Bombardier or no Bombardier. And I'm aching to see the fun."

"But how shall we manage it?" Faced with the need for action, Tommy could never think what to do, rather in the way that when he tried to write, the words would refuse to come; and one of the things that made Felix so mysterious and admirable in his eyes was that he suffered from no such disability.

"Do it up in a neat parcel, enclosing your card, and present it to this utterly splendid Prado of yours."

At the very idea of such a thing, the patriot's natural timorousness returned in a great rush. "I couldn't enclose my card," he exclaimed, omitting to mention that he had none. "If I did that, I might lose my job."

"Then how, my hero, will your glory ever shine forth?"

"Oh, everyone will know," Tommy assured him. "Everyone always knows everything in Dublin. But not officially, if you see what I mean. I could always deny it. And there's the Organization to be thought of, too."

"A lot it worries about you!"

"Ah, now, now," Tommy said. "There'll be something behind all that."

But the thought of presenting the canvas to the Prado, an enterprise on a scale in keeping with his own exploit, appealed to him very much. After further consultation, it was agreed that this should be done, anonymously and with Felix acting as messenger.

They now went up to the attic to find the picture. Someone had removed the makeshift wrappings, and had parceled it beautifully up in new brown paper and string, writing "Afrodisio Lafuente" in Irish lettering across one corner. It could only have been the work of Mrs. Barry, a little mark of her respect and interest that touched them both. Next came the question of where the delivery should be made. Pending the completion of the Temple of Art itself, all communications for it were sent to a box-office number, arranged, of course, by Tacky, and they thought in the present case to approach it through this would be undignified and unsuitable. They decided that it should be addressed to The Director of the Irish Temple of Art, c/o The Committee for the Irish Temple of Art, and that Felix should seek out Mr. Mervyn Roche and hand it over in person.

"Don't get into conversation about it, mind," Tommy warned him.

As a rule, the pans and kettles of the showroom and the housewives, peevish or arch, who wandered in and out were a grievous affliction to Tommy. He thought them unworthy of an Irish patriot, who also wrote plays. The brusque voice of his employer, Mr. Pye, usually grated on his ear like a false note on the piano. Today he noticed none of these things, but went about his duties in a kind of trance. His soul was full of the solemn yet burning exultation that he had experienced when taking his leave of the Bombardier: an exultation, indeed, still greater, for then he had merely been a soldier pledged in a cause and now he was the warrior returned and victorious, with the laurels about to be placed on his head. He lived so much in his dreams that the translation of this particularly noble one into reality appeared almost miraculous. He had to keep telling himself of it, or he would not have believed it was true.

I really did it, he whispered, I really did. Really, really.

All at once he became distantly aware that someone was speaking to him, and glancing around, saw that it was Mr. Pye. His employer's red face was redder than usual and there was unmistakable menace in the glare of his light blue eyes. He was waving the list of yesterday's sales that Tommy had to compile every morning before he did anything else. The typist in her little glass cage was tittering in the empty way she had.

"Well?" demanded Mr. Pye.

"I beg your pardon, sir?" said the startled Tommy.

"Are you deaf, boy? For the third time, what in thunder do you mean by sending in a list like this?

I can't make head or tail of it. Four Morgans! What is a Morgan at all?"

"Casseroles, I should have said, sir."

Mr. Pye dealt him a terrible look and returned to the study of the list. Suddenly his bushy brows shot up his forehead, giving him an almost demented air. "And look here!" he screamed. "It's dated the fifteenth of Ireland!"

"May, sir, May."

Mr. Pye suddenly found a quiet composure that was more horrifying than his rage. He folded the list up and put it away in a waistcoat pocket as if it were a valuable document, speaking meanwhile to his alarmed employee in a gentle, compassionate tone: "I am afraid, O'Driscoll, you have not yet recovered from your indisposition."

"What indisposition was that, sir?" Tommy asked in real surprise.

Mr. Pye looked at him lovingly. "The one that deprived us of your impressive help last Monday, O'Driscoll. The third in six weeks. I'm afraid we are overworking you." He uncovered his tobacco-stained teeth in a grin of pleasure. "Fair play for you, though. Now you shall have a holiday. Don't thank me—" He smiled, as Tommy's face grew bright. "A long, long holiday. As long as you like. In fact, you can take your hat and begin it now. Your wages, with an extra week in lieu, will be sent to you at home."

Tommy had been expecting something of the sort for a while past. It was a favorite boast of his that he had a kind of sixth sense for impending misfortune. He had even gone so far as to rehearse in his mind an impassioned appeal for another chance, to be made when the blow should fall. Now was the moment to make that appeal, and yet he said nothing. It was as if a higher self forbade him, in this his finest hour, to grovel before this vulgar, mindless man, so typical of the Ireland of today, so unworthy of the Ireland of the past: one of the blind, unthinking mob for whom—O irony—he had nevertheless been prepared to hazard all. He put on his hat and raincoat, took his umbrella and his luncheon packet, and went to the door, where he paused.

"This is the sort of thing, Mr. Pye, that breeds communism."

And, with a fine, sad dignity, he swept out.

Later on, as he sat munching his sandwiches on a bench in St. Stephen's Green, he had a drop in mood. Cold, horrible fact penetrated his mind like a blade of steel. He had no job. What would become of him? Beside this calamity, even the wrongs of Ireland dwindled away into nothing. He would not be able to find another post, for Mr. Pye would never recommend him. Was it too late even now to go back and apologize, plead illness, worry or trouble at home? That sixth sense of his replied that it was. Desperately he tried to find some cheering element in the situation. He told himself that at least the non-payment of his rent would be regularized by the change in his circumstances. And Felix now need never know that he had worked in a shop; he had always described his employment to this elegant friend as "something in the City" and often at night would turn hot and cold in his bed at the idea of the truth leaking out. He reminded himself that to get two weeks' wages together would give him a little capital to play with. He could say, too, that he had lost his job through devotion to Ireland, possibly to Mr. Pye's detriment; and if the worst came to the worst, could he marry money perhaps? None of it really convinced or encouraged him, however, and at last with a heavy heart he set out for home.

As a rule it gave him pleasure to come back to the house in the evening. The sweep of blue hills in the background, the flowers and trees in the garden, the chattering of the brook in the meadow beyond revived his spirits; and after the petty humiliations and vexations of the day it soothed him to turn in at the wide gates and to walk down the drive toward the large, handsome building as if he owned it. As often as not he would find a few brown eggs on the hall stand, or some butter or vegetables, put there for him by the Landlord; or she would be there herself, her blue eyes twinkling, to make him laugh with some wild tale of happenings in the village.

Now, arriving home disgraced in the middle of the afternoon, he felt quite differently. There was no one about. Mrs. Barry, he knew, had gone to have tea with the local Rector; and Felix had apparently not yet returned. There was a curious atmosphere in the house, as if it were watching him and laughing to itself. It seemed in a horrible way to be in the know. He hung up his raincoat and hurried out into the garden.

Peadar had taken advantage of the Landlord's absence to invite company in for the afternoon. His friend was a scarecrow like himself, with big blue eyes very close together in a sooty face that gave him the air of a low comedian. The pair of them were settled on the wooden boxes in the shelter of a wall, drinking Mrs. Barry's beer out of Mrs. Barry's Waterford glass, and gazing thoughtfully at a crop of dande-lion.

"I don't know a bit where would Mr. Horniman be," he said in answer to Tommy's inquiry. "I'd have to ask me assistant."

The assistant was a new acquisition of Peadar's, and made his life run much more smoothly. He had begged Mrs. Barry's permission to employ him, say-ing that his health left much to be desired these days, while his brain had never been of the first class. It would not cost her a penny, for he would pay the man's wages from his own; but it would be a comfort to him, getting on in years as he was, to be able to share his responsibility. In fact, the assistant existed only in Peadar's imagination, his role being that of scapegoat.

"Ah, it's that fellow again, ma'am," he would say nowadays, in response to the Landlord's reproaches. "I wonder, is he a Christian at all?"

Since the arrangement came into being, Peadar was looking a good deal happier in himself, the fact that Mrs. Barry was not deceived, and that Peadar had never supposed she would be, making no difference to either.

"Then would you be kind enough to do that?" asked Tommy, eyeing the shabby old man with con-tempt.

"Ah, sure, I couldn't," Peadar replied, unmoved. "He's off to the hills this evening again, without a word. Oh, he's a terror!"

There was a glint of laughter in the octopus eyes of the scarecrow that provoked the young man ex-tremely; but his time was too valuable to waste on a humbug like Peadar. Turning his back on the men, he marched off to the house again, ignoring the subdued chuckles that arose in the rear. He did not begin to worry at once about Felix being away, because his friend, of course, imagined he would still be at work. Nor would he bother to telephone, as Mrs. Barry regarded that instrument as merely for use when she wanted to ring up herself, and Peadar never went near it at all, being afraid for his life of upsetting it. Very few messages ever filtered through in that household. But six o'clock came, and then seven, and there was no Felix; and now Tommy did begin to feel very anxious indeed. How frightful it would be if an accident were to befall a man as rich as that, and so free with his money! By this time he had grown accustomed to Felix's taking him about in the Daimler and giving him wonderful meals in restaurants that he had never expected to enter. He felt no embarrassment at all at Felix's invariably paying for them, which he looked on as a form of restitution for the wrongs committed by England in the past. It had been a crumb of comfort in his dreadful new predicament to know that Felix would be at his side.

All through that long evening he waited for his friend as a girl waits for a lover. He would hold his breath and listen for the sound of the motorcar; every few moments he ran to the window to look, and once he went up to the road itself and watched for his coming there. The ancient clocks in the house, all telling different times, jerked slowly on. At last from the parish church he heard the hour of eleven strike, and all hope died away. His sixth sense told him that something terrible had happened, that Felix was dead. It was a gift, or a curse, in his family to know of such events without being apprised of them, his mother had always told him: it was the mark of the true Gael.

He would never see Felix again; and at the thought of this he was overwhelmed by a grief that was utterly pure, freeing him in its intensity from the small concerns and calculations that wormed about in his brain. Nothing now mattered beside the fact of that blithe creature lying cold and still in some hospital mortuary. Tommy clasped his hands and bowed his head in prayer; and even as he did so he heard the purr of the Daimler as it swung into the garden. Then the engine stopped and the door opened, and a light, familiar voice was raised in song. With an abrupt change of mood Tommy went downstairs with the lowering face of a wife about to greet a truant husband. Felix was just coming into the house, his face flushed and his hat on the back of his head.

"What-ho! What-ho! What-ho! It's in the bag!" he caroled.

"You took your time," was all that Tommy would say, and that in the sourest possible voice.

eight

Felix was taken aback by the cool reception of his news. He had carried out a difficult task in what seemed to him an exemplary manner. First he had looked up Mr. Mervyn Roche in the telephone book and driven directly to the only address he found there. This was of an office in Anglesea Street, a curiously Victorian establishment, with high stools and dusty ledgers and on the walls a number of old prints of people engaged in hunting, skating, carol-singing and other reassuring pursuits. But even as this was the only office Tacky listed, so it was the one he really never used; he would have prevented his left hand knowing what his right one was up to had he been able, and the peevish old clerk, with his spectacles pushed up on his forehead, disclaimed all knowledge of his movements.

"We don't see him that often" was all he would say.

Felix pleaded and scolded, and at last the clerk reluctantly gave him a list of Tacky's other haunts, which he proceeded to draw one by one; and in the third of them was rewarded by the information that Mr. Roche was at present attending a Requiem Mass for a celebrated temperance worker in a church down on the quays. If he made haste he should be able to intercept him as he came out.

"And what does he look like?" Felix inquired.

"Ah well, that's hard to say," his informant said cautiously. "If you saw him once, you'd never forget it; but I can't put it nearer than that. Sure, anyone'll point him out. He's very well known."

With some misgiving Felix drove at high speed to the church in question, where a trickle of mourners was already coming through the somber hangings at the door. The temperance worker had been cut down in the prime of life, and the subdued expression on some of the richly colored faces was mingled with a certain complacency. Grasping the picture, Felix ran up the steps and without ceremony begged the nearest man to help him. Mr. Roche would hardly be out just yet, he was told, since, as one of the chief mourners, he had been right up in the front. With growing excitement Felix waited there while the worshipers streamed past, deputies, stockbrokers, bank managers, lawyers, the elite of Dublin, wishing each other good day with the nervous affability of men who have been reminded of death.

"Now! There's Mervyn Roche!" the man said as Tacky came forward in splendid black, his head still bare and with a look of honest grief on his face.

"I hardly like to worry him now," Felix demurred, noting this and suddenly remembering his manners.

"Ah, for God's sake!" The man was immensely tickled by something.

Unwilling as he was to intrude at such a moment, Felix could see no help for it. If once he allowed his quarry to get away, who knew when he would find him again? And too much was at stake for hazards of the kind. He therefore followed the bowed figure at a respectful distance until it made to enter a Rolls Royce that waited across the road; then he put on a spurt and, removing his own hat, said in a gentle, sympathetic tone, "Mr. Roche? May I have a word with you, sir?"

Tacky wheeled about, his demeanor marvelously altered. There was a spark of irritation in his close-set eyes which, however, died away as he observed Felix's expensive attire. Next he treated the young man to a wary, penetrating look as if he were both divining his intention and warning him to think better of it. After that he glanced hurriedly around to see who was within earshot. At last the wide mouth stretched in a flashing smile of welcome, while the eyes above remained cold and steady as a mountain lake. In all this he merely followed his normal practice when strangers accosted him.

"You may, of course," he said effusively. "As many as you like!"

"I am instructed to give you this, sir," Felix said dramatically, "on behalf of an Irish patriot." And, pushing his sacred charge into Tacky's hand, he walked rapidly away, jumped into the Daimler and drove off to the Royal Hibernian without looking back. It only remained to telephone the Dublin newspapers one by one and inform them, as from a well-wisher who preferred to remain incognito, of what had taken place; he did so immediately on reaching his Club, afterwards going in to luncheon with a happy sense of a morning well spent.

Being uncertain how long the search for Tacky would require, he had made no plans for the afternoon; and he now began to consider ways in which it might be agreeably passed. It came into his mind that dear old Freddie was said to be working in the British Embassy here. Dear old Freddie had been his inseparable companion at school, a bright, handsome boy of the same happy and fun-loving temperament as himself. When the time came to leave, the two of them had sworn eternal friendship and mutual support in case of need, and had undertaken to meet once a year even if half the world lay between them. Since then they had run into each other half a dozen times, and always with pleasure to both. Felix thought he could not do better than look dear Freddie up and renew this pleasant association; and the thought of the role himself was playing in Anglo-Irish affairs lent a particular spice to the idea.

He smiled wickedly to himself in the Embassy waiting room as he sat under a portrait of the Duke of Edinburgh, with an ancient number of *Country Life* on his knee. But when the attendant came back, saying that Mr. Davenport would see him at once, and showed him into Freddie's room, his friend's appearance drove everything else from his head. For one terrible moment he thought it was due to age, and that he himself must affect the people he met in the same way. In the next, his common sense returned and he understood, with a great welling-up of the compassion that was so peculiarly his, that this was what happened to men who were obliged to work for their living. But for the grace of God, those haggard looks, that thinning hair, might have been his own lot; and, overcome by a noble pity, he stretched out his hand without a word.

"Is it really you, Felix? Are you really here?" said Mr. Davenport brokenly. "How wonderful. How wonderful."

He could not say more, as the telephone began to ring and he picked it up as if waiting for it to explode, staring huntedly around the room meanwhile. "Hallo? Ah. No, don't put him on, don't put him on, Miss Bostock," he cried urgently. "Have you explained that we have no powers in the matter? Well, what does he say? The Embassy *what?* Oh, really! No, I will not have lunch with him, tomorrow or ever. Tell him his best plan is to write to the editor again himself. And Miss Bostock! No more calls until further notice, please. I am in conference."

He put the receiver down and fell back into his chair, motioning to Felix to take another.

"That was Professor O'Malley," he said with a quiet sadness that pierced his friend to the heart. "*The Times* has not printed a letter of his. He believes that His Excellency has privately requested them not to. He says it is well known we compile a black list of Irishmen whose views are not to be published. He wants to meet me and talk it over."

"Explosive stuff, the letter, I dare say?" Felix asked sympathetically.

Freddie gave a sudden, horrifying laugh. "It was a description, running to fifteen hundred words, of a king's tomb recently excavated at Nenagh." He opened a box of cigarettes and pushed it across the desk to Felix with hands that noticeably trembled.

"Do you get much of this sort of thing?" Felix inquired, still in the bedside manner.

"You have no idea," Freddie answered. "No one

has any idea. Look at that, for instance," and he passed him a torn sheet of paper covered with crude writing.

" 'You dirty, skulking bastards,' " Felix read, " 'get out of Ireland and go back to the flea-pits over the water where you belong. You stinkers, you pollute the earth of this Christian land. . . .' Bless my soul, though, Freddie, that's a bit steep, isn't it? Perhaps he doesn't really mean it."

"That file," proceeded Freddie, indicating a large box on the corner of the desk, "is crammed full of similar communications."

"Would they soften toward you at all, do you think, if they knew you kept their letters?"

"I keep them only," Freddie assured him, "lest I ever soften myself. If ever my brain gives way, as I daily expect, and I begin babbling about Irish charm and Irish kindness and smiling Irish eyes, a quick refresher course with that file should save me."

"Come, I don't like to see you so bitter," Felix said with a touch of reproof. "This isn't the little old Freddie I used to know. And I fear you are exaggerating somewhat."

"Do you think so, Felix?"

"I do indeed."

There was a knock at the door and the attendant came in, closing it carefully and mysteriously behind him. "He's here, sir," he murmured. "Shall I say you are engaged?"

"By no means, Gallagher," Freddie said with a sudden, artificial brightness. "Show him in, if you will. I think Mr. Horniman should meet him. Exaggerating, eh?" he remarked softly and venomously to Felix as the servant went out.

The person who now came slowly into the room,

leaning on a cane with a silver top, made an instant impression on Felix. Everything about him seemed to say that here was a remarkable character. The head was fine, surmounted by a luxuriant crop of white hair; the eyes, large and dark and wide apart, shone as if reflecting to the world outside a fire that raged within. More striking even than these was the immense dignity with which he bore himself, a dignity behind which there waited, clearly and not unattractively, a limitless arrogance. As he caught sight of the visitor a haughty frown came over his face, and he stopped, leaning with both great hands on the cane and fixing Mr. Davenport with a look of peculiar intensity.

"I had expected to find you alone," he began in a deep, resonant voice. "My business is private."

"You may speak freely before Mr. Horniman," Freddie declared, addressing him with the utmost courtesy. "We have no secrets from him. And he will never divulge what he hears between these walls."

"So you may say," the stranger grumbled. "So you may say. But how can I trust you? You know the matter on which I have come. It is the same as I had the honor of putting before you last week, and the week before that. And you have done nothing. You promised that steps would be taken, and you have done nothing. They are still there, following me wherever I go. My every move is noted down, and that, I say, at your instigation. How could it be otherwise?" His manner had been growing more and more agitated as he spoke, and now he appeared to forget that Felix was present. Taking a step forward, he continued: "True, there was the bomb. But all that is past and done. Are bygones never to be bygones? I have done you no injury. Am I never to know a moment's peace of mind again? I tell you, I cannot endure it!" he shouted, putting a hand to his temple.

"I will go into the matter at once," Mr. Davenport assured him suavely, "and if I find your complaint is justified, be sure I will endeavor to put things right."

"Wherever I go!" the old man cried. "Shrieking and swooping! There was one on my window sill this morning, watching me as I lay in bed."

"Leave it in my hands," Mr. Davenport said in the soothing voice of someone talking to a frightened child, "and come along with me. I'll send you home in the Embassy car; you'll be safe there, at all events." And still murmuring phrases of comfort, he escorted the visitor from the room.

"Exaggerating, eh?" he repeated on his return.

"My dear soul, I do believe I shall have to apologize!" Felix exclaimed. "Do tell me what on earth all that was about."

"I will."

The story that Mr. Davenport had to unfold was sufficiently out of the common; and he told it in a matter-of-fact sort of way that was more impressive than any flourishes could have been. Some months ago the Embassy had received an unsigned letter, notifying them of a plot to bomb the building and giving details of where the bomb was at present being manufactured. As a matter of routine, they had passed the letter to the Civic Guards; and as a matter of routine the Civic Guards had raided the premises in question. There was nothing unusual in the affair up to this, but from now on it grew very strange. To their astonishment, the Guards had in fact discovered an old man on the spot, hard at work on a bomb. They had arrested him, at the same time removing the bomb and certain papers they found lying about. An officer of the Irish Army was called in to examine and dismantle the offensive machine, which he soon was able to declare was harmless, being filled with coffee grounds and having a bootlace for fuse. Still more puzzling was the fact, established by the Guards after a patient scrutiny of the impounded documents, that the old man himself had written the letter of warning. They had loyally reported their findings to the Embassy, but in the briefest way, and had been extremely evasive when asked to account for these curious procedures.

Shortly after the incident Mr. Davenport had been informed that a visitor had called, insisting on an interview with someone in authority but declining to give his name or reveal the nature of his business. It was the old man whom Felix had just seen—who, with indescribable distress, had admitted to being the plotter. He was more sorry than words could say for what he had done. But was it right, he inquired piteously, was it just or merciful, that the Embassy should hound him forever? Was it English fair play, putting the Dublin sea gulls on him, to follow him around the town and spy him out, to pass remarks about him in their wild, terrible voices and madden him with their pitiless laughter? Freddie had conducted this delicate interview as best he could, immediately afterwards setting an inquiry in train; and in due course the Embassy learned who and what the old man was. These visits had now become a weekly event and, said Freddie, with a sudden casting aside of his nonchalant manner, he did not know how much longer he could bear it.

"Steady, steady! He's barking, that's all," Felix said. "Why don't they lock the poor old fellow up?"

"His brother is a Bishop," was the simple reply.

"All right. But why see him? Why not just be out?"

"His brother is a Bishop, I tell you," said Freddie, raising his voice impatiently.

"Well, then, couldn't the Bishop be asked to do something?"

Mr. Davenport gave one of his dreadful laughs.

Now Felix grew seriously perturbed about this friend of his. It had been harrowing enough to find him in such pitiable shape on first being shown to his room; but that anyone should continue despondent, and even distracted, after half an hour or so of his company struck him as positively unnatural. He could remember nothing like it before. That smiling faces should greet him wherever he went was as much, to his mind, a law of creation as that he should drive about in a Daimler. Yet, if he were nonplused by an element of mystery in the situation itself, he felt no doubts at all as to its cure.

"What do you say to worrying a bone at Jammet's later on?" he suggested. "And a thoughtful noggin or so at the Club afterwards? We may be able to get things into perspective."

"Oh, it's gone far beyond that," was the tragic reply; but the sufferer allowed himself to be persuaded, stipulating only that Felix should meet him at his own Club beforehand. He left his office never later than five and was into his second or third drink by six; in this way only, he asserted, could the remains of his sanity be preserved.

The evening bore witness to the soundness of the Horniman philosophy. Gradually as time went by, Mr. Davenport emerged from the shadows of despair and became the light-hearted soul that Felix had known. Felix himself was so happy to see it, and everything was so pleasant, that all else went out of his head and it was not until after ten that he remembered the events of the day and the patriot waiting for news at home.

"Good Heavens! I must go at once," he exclaimed. "You'll never guess what I've been at." It now occurred to him, relaxed as he was, that dear old Freddie should be told about it. To conceal matters of importance from dear old Freddie, at this stage of the evening, was unthinkably disloyal. Fighting Ireland's battles for her was all great fun, but he had not been at school with Ireland; and he therefore blurted the story out, beginning it from the moment that Tommy's path had crossed his own. Mr. Davenport heard him with strained attention, and his response at the end came as something of a surprise.

"Thank God!" he cried fervently. "Of course. Of course. Oh, Felix, what a weight off my mind!"

"You ought to be shocked, though, oughtn't you?"

"Damn what I ought to be," was the answer. "You don't know what this means. Because, my dear boy," he said, with great earnestness, "don't you see that if the story had been true as told, they would have had more guts and more imagination than I ever supposed. Which is absurd. Which is preposterous."

"But you mustn't breathe a word."

"It would be a waste of time if I did," Freddie assured him. "Another terrible beauty is born . . ." He broke off abruptly and began to laugh, a long, deep, satisfying laugh that seemed to well up from the very core of his being. "You good man," he said feebly, when at last he could speak. "You good, good man."

With this opinion, harmonizing as it did with his own, echoing in his ears, with the wine singing in his veins and with his heart full of the satisfaction of duties ably and honestly performed, Felix now returned to the house—to be greeted by the white-faced Tommy, whose only comment was that he'd taken his time! But Felix was above all petty resentment.

"I'm a shocker," he cheerfully agreed. "But what do you think? After I gave the picture to Mr. Roche, I fell in with an old, old chum who's in the British Embassy here. We simply had to dine, you know, after all these years. What an evening we've had! The things he told me! And, of course, I told him all about the picture. He laughed like a madman."

Tommy found the remark immensely irritating. Everything about Felix irritated him just at that moment: his clothes, his accent, his money, his lightness of heart, the ease with which he had apparently dealt with the picture and his frivolity in going off on the spree afterwards. It angered him, too, to think how he had watched and suffered while this playboy was regaling an official representative of the enemy with their secret; and that the enemy should laugh at what ought to have filled him with impotent rage.

"He's a queer sense of humor, then," he said. "An Irishman would never do that. No wonder your Empire is crumbling."

"Empires do," said Felix merrily. "It's a little way of theirs. Be glad you never got one."

"Who says we didn't?" said Tommy fiercely. "Our Empire is spiritual and intellectual and extends all over the world. It existed already when you fellows were running about painted blue. Yours was a little tinpot affair of guns and Bibles and trade." His hands began to shake, and he thrust them viciously into his trouser pockets.

At this moment the front door opened again to admit the Landlord carrying a lamp, a spear and a basket of fish. After a couple of hours' harpooning on a lonely strip of the shore, she was still fresh and gay and alert, and at once, as she was wont, uttered the thought that happened to cross her mind without regard for its absolute relevance.

"Extraordinary, the people one meets nowadays," she commented. "Such a funny little woman at tea today. The Rector mentioned that I had been in India, and she asked what Indians were like! 'I'm afraid I never met any,' I told her—I hope, not unkindly."

With a muttered exclamation Tommy turned on his heel and rushed upstairs to the attic, slamming the door behind him.

"Now what in the world is wrong with that one?" Mrs. Barry wanted to know.

Felix only wished he could tell her. He began to feel that the day had been somewhat crowded and that his best plan was to get some rest; he was in no shape at the moment to start fathoming the national psyche. Having carried the Landlord's fish to the kitchen and wiped her gory spear, he chatted lightly to her about members of the Irish landed gentry while she boiled herself an egg; and as soon as he decently could, retired to his room. As he thankfully climbed into bed, however, there was a timid knock on the door and Tommy appeared, with the forlorn and childlike air he had had at their first encounter.

"I thought you'd an accident," he said in a rush. "I was sitting here thinking you might be dead. That is why I passed that remark about the Empire.

You won't understand in a thousand years, but I wanted to tell you. And I was rude to Mrs. Barry because I thought what she said about Indians was intended for me. Our cruel history has made us sensitive," he concluded with a quiet lucidity that set the other man's brain reeling.

"Your cruel history hasn't made you an Indian, has it?"

Tommy allowed himself to smile. "I love your crazy way of looking at things," he said benevolently. Yielding again to his desire for clarification, he went on: "I have the honor to inform you that today I lost my job. I worked in a shop, selling pots. Don't mind what I told you before. And it made me angry, too, to think of you despising me for it. I mean, if you had known. And having dinner and laughing like that, when I thought you were killed. I'm not saying it was your fault." He sighed and passed a thin hand over his eyes. "You'll be tired now. I won't torment you. I only wanted to explain, in case you were wondering."

Softly closing the door he crept away to his attic, leaving the puzzled Felix to stare up into the darkness.

nine

"Excellent, of its kind," Lady Twomey declared emphatically.

"Unobjectionable," said Miss Scully with reluctance.

"A bloody mess, if you ask me," said Seumas Cullen. He used this description of any work that did not resemble his own.

"I had expected something larger," Mr. MacMahon complained.

"What's it supposed to be?" inquired Mr. Connolly.

The Committee, hastily convened yet again, were sitting in front of the celebrated picture. The meeting place this time was a strong-room especially constructed for one of Tacky's more intimate enterprises, and the fact that they were allowed in it at all was a measure of the solemnity of the occasion. With its steel doors and barred windows, it had the cheerless effect of a cell, the more so as Tacky had stowed away every scrap of paper and movable object in the safe before the visitors came. His one concession had been to leave an oleograph of the "Infant of Prague" on the wall. He was looking tired and careworn, and not at all like his usual ebullient self; the problem he had so lightly put before his colleagues the other day was one he had never dreamed might arise.

"Ladies and gentlemen, that is not the point," he said, wearily smoothing his hair. "The history of this picture is such as to make its artistic qualities a minor consideration. I have told you all how it came into my hands yesterday. What I ask now is guidance in the way of procedure. I can't hold the Press off forever."

"Isn't it a matter for the Government?" asked Mr. MacMahon.

"He says it isn't," Tacky ruefully answered, "unless and until the English Embassy makes a formal dee-march. You see the point, of course; he's looking for a quiet way out. He wants to keep the affair as between the Morgan Gallery and the Temple of Art. I'm afraid we're out on a limb."

The faces of the other men in the room grew long.

"These things are tricky all right," said Mr. Mac-Mahon gloomily. "Common sense flies out of the window when patriotism comes in at the door. Not that I'm against patriotism," he added at once.

"Legally, we haven't a leg to stand on," Tacky proceeded. "I'd a word with one of the judges last evening. We can do the legal thing and send it back. I don't have to tell you what the country would say to that. We can do the just and proper thing and please the country, but annoy the people across the water—

and some of us have connections there"—Tacky
looked unusually self-conscious as he said this—"*and
run the risk of being slapped down by the Government after all at the finish.*"

It was rare indeed for Tacky to express his thoughts
so fully and plainly; and this again was a measure of
the gravity of the situation.

"Couldn't you tip off the English Embassy, in an
anonymous kind of way?" Mr. Connolly suggested.
"They'd have to approach the Government then."

"That has been done," the Chairman informed
him with a pitying glance.

"I have it!" said Lady Twomey. "Why not send it
to the House of Irish Painting?"

A little murmur of admiration greeted her words.
The House was a small gallery, within easy reach of
the Palace Bar, reserved entirely for works by living
Irish artists. In a modest way, it had experienced the
same difficulty in covering its walls as now confronted
the Irish Prado; indeed, had it not been for the new
and vigorous Sallynoggin Group, which in the nick of
time had revived the style and scale of Delacroix, it
might have had to think of closing down altogether.
When the fuss about the Lafuente picture first began, therefore, it had announced with alacrity that
one of its rooms should be kept standing perpetually
bare, in protest. The Municipal Gallery kept a room
similarly bare in respect of the Lane pictures, un-
justly retained by the English, too, on the grounds of
some legal quibble; so that the gesture of the House
struck everyone as appropriate, dignified and practical.

"We could ask them," Lady Twomey proceeded,
"to house the painting as a special exhibit, pending a
final settlement as to the ownership."

"Excellent! I'll second that," said Mr. MacMahon. "They ought to be pleased. It'll attract a crowd of people there, and they'll have no responsibility."

Tacky vigorously rubbed his hands. "Lady Twomey, I declare you're worth two of me," he exclaimed. "I'd never have thought of it. That way we're covered all round. It's a masterpiece!"

"Ah, but wait now," Miss Scully put in. "What if Ireland finally keeps the picture and the crowd down there refuse to hand it back to us?" Like many a fervent nationalist, she had the lowest possible opinion of her countrymen.

"I'm surprised at you," Lady Twomey said, the loftier standards of Birmingham implicit in her tone.

"Forewarned is forearmed."

"I'm sure they would never do anything so despicable," Tacky said, "and anyway I have means of bringing pressure. No; I'll have a word with them and as soon as we fix things up I'll release the story to the Press. Then I will send a formal letter to the Morgan Gallery, setting out the position and requesting their views. Pass the buck, in fact. They'd hardly have the temerity to refuse us justice in black and white!"

"I'll bet anyone here a dollar we don't see the picture again." Miss Scully was not to be mollified.

"Time enough to cross our bridges when we come to them!"

One more meeting extraordinary of the Committee for the Irish Temple of Art was over. Lady Twomey went on to the Beaux Arts Club in the hope of a game of bridge with some of the wives of dentists and attorneys who formed its principal membership. Seumas Cullen returned to his studio and resumed work on his "Sligo Mother." Mr. Connolly dropped into a Turf Accountant's Office. Mr. Mac-

Mahon hurried away to one of his own auctions, to
stimulate the bidding. Miss Scully did the Stations
of the Cross in a chapel and then went home; her key
was in the front door before she remembered she was
out of Courvoisier. Tacky applied himself to the task
in hand at once.

The House of Irish Painting was more generously
co-operative than even Tacky had dared to hope. Certain little provisos were made, in order to protect itself, and there was an understanding, not the less
definite for being unspoken, that at some future and
appropriate time there should be a *quid pro quo*.
But it was clear that the notion appealed to it
strongly. With the coming of the warm weather
and the long evenings, the attendance, never great,
tended to fall away, and there were days when a
workless man, a colored student or two, or some tormented soul who wished to be alone, were the only
people to pass the door. The acquisition of a plum
like the Afrodisio Lafuente would change all that in
the twinkling of an eye, particularly if England behaved in the brutal and grasping way expected of her
and the whole affair blossomed out as yet another
glorious national issue.

"What's the picture like, by the way?" someone
asked as an afterthought, as Tacky prepared to take
his leave.

"I haven't really looked at it yet," Tacky admitted.
"There's a desperate amount of red and yellow, but
my experts do say it's the finest the man ever did."

All that now remained was to write the letter to
the Morgan Gallery, and release the news to the papers. After that Tacky drove out to a villa he had at
Dalkey, judging that reporters would make his town
house uninhabitable for the next forty-eight hours.

Having mixed himself a strong Irish and water, he sank down on a sofa and let his eye wander complacently about the room, the chairs with their fine lace backs, the expensive china ornaments, the holy pictures and the photographs of horses. He had got out of the fix by what was almost a miracle. The next move was England's; and the last thing he wanted at present was to quarrel with anyone or to champion any cause on earth. For the twentieth time since yesterday morning he felt inside his waistcoat pocket for a certain newspaper cutting, and for the twentieth time read it over.

It was a short description of the recent activities of his son, who had taken a degree at Oxford the year before and was at present living in London on a princely allowance while he considered his future. Patrick Mervyn was Tacky's only child and the apple of his eye. It was for him that he toiled early and late, never sparing himself or minding the hard words of those he overreached; and this he did in the purest spirit of love, asking nothing and expecting nothing but that his boy should live as a gentleman, should enjoy the good things that he had been denied himself. Fondly his eye now rested on the few lines of print. The Honorable John Massingham-Slade! The Honorable Simon Biscocque! Martin Soames, the nephew of a Duke! Such, it was stated in black and white, were his Paddy's boon companions. True, the story itself left something to be desired; the Magistrate, indeed, had gone so far as to say the case was one of the worst to come before him. All very drunk, the young men had broken into a lady's house by mistake, taking it for one belonging to a friend with whom they were displeased, and had chopped her furniture to bits with axes. Only their youth had saved them from prison; the fines were enormous, and so would the damages be. Ah, but boys will be boys, Tacky thought, reverently tucking the paper away again; sure, anyone could make an error of judgment with a few jars inside of him.

"The Honorable John Massingham-Slade!" he murmured, rolling the words around his tongue. "The Honorable Simon Biscocque!"

On a table beside him were two photographs, in silver frames, of the late Mrs. Mervyn Roche. One of them, faded and brown, showed her as a slender girl in a homemade wedding dress, modestly holding a bouquet of lilies of the valley to her face. From the other, taken in the year of her death, smiled a fat, resolute matron wearing a black lace gown and any number of bangles and beads. Tacky's eyes grew moist as he considered them each in turn. Mary should have been here to see this crowning of all their efforts, this justification of their existence; this proof, too, of his own perspicacity, for she had always declared that to send Paddy to Oxford was a shocking waste of money. She wanted to know what was wrong with the National. Nothing, of course, except that you wouldn't meet Honorables there: Onorables, as he must remember to call them. He began to picture her on a visit to London in brand-new finery. But then it occurred to him to wonder would she have been at her ease with Paddy's fine friends, and what sort of figure would she have cut there at all, and he suspected that as usual Providence had acted for the best.

"She's better off where she is, please God," he murmured, devoutly raising his eyes to the ceiling as he spoke.

Meanwhile, as Tacky had foreseen, the reporters

were ranging to and fro in the city like hounds that have not yet picked up a trail. All who could have made an authoritative pronouncement had suddenly and mysteriously gone to earth. Even the British Embassy denied all knowledge of the affair beyond what had already appeared in the papers. Accordingly, the Pressmen determined to split up and track down the members of the Committee one by one, meeting again later on to compare their notes. It was a confused little conference that was finally held, as only Lady Twomey had given a plain account of the Committee's action; the remarks of the men were so guarded as to be incomprehensible, while Miss Scully, who was halfway through her bottle when the reporter arrived, had muddled the issue with a previous one and burst forth on the subject of obscene paintings with the fire of a Redemptorist.

At the same time, nevertheless, the news was spreading through surer channels than the official ones that the picture was now at the House of Irish Painting and would be on exhibit within a few days.

Mr. Paul O'Farrell waited indoors, anxiously expecting the telephone to ring. As he saw it, a crucial point was reached. If he were still the strong favorite for the Directorship, someone surely must approach him now and informally seek his views on the new development. If nobody did, it could only mean that O'Hara was well in the running. To a man of his lucid mind no other explanation was admissible.

No one telephoned because no one knew how to pronounce "Lafuente y Chaos," and no one was going to make a fool of himself if he could help it. At last Mr. O'Farrell could bear the silence no longer, and testily clapping on his sombrero, he marched off to the House of Irish Painting itself, where he subjected a huge canvas entitled "Cabra Allotments" to a patient scrutiny it had never received before. Like Tacky, the man in charge had promptly retired into hiding, but, tipped off by the typist, he immediately sent an apprentice to deal with the illustrious visitor. On seeing Mr. O'Farrell, the youth gave a cry of surprise and delight.

"Well, this is a pleasure all right, Mr. O'Farrell," he exclaimed. "It's a long time that we didn't see you."

"I do not get to the collections as often as I could wish," Mr. O'Farrell replied sonorously, his tone implying that the collections were much to be pitied.

"It's well you got here today, then. We were just going to ring you up."

"Indeed?" asked Mr. O'Farrell, all marvelously at sea, but with a quickening of the pulse.

"Would you ever come with me a moment?" He led the way to a small private room where a picture, swathed in cloth, stood on an easel. "What do you say to this one?" he asked, whipping the cloth away.

Mr. O'Farrell pursed his lips and with half-closed eyes studied the painting attentively for a while.

"Undoubtedly, Lafuente y Chaos," he said at last. "A fine specimen of the early-middle period. You have observed the treatment of the light in relation to the animal's hide. I think we must say 1913; I think we dare not put it earlier than that."

"Right as a trivet!" cried the youth. "God, Mr. O'Farrell, there's no one like you. That's just what it is: the famous Goat picture that La . . . La . . . the painter bequeathed to Ireland."

"Not the one there was all the fuss about?" Mr. O'Farrell asked in astonishment.

"The very one!"

"Bless my soul. And what is it doing here?"

"Do you mean to say you didn't hear?"

"I am out of touch with events, I fear," Mr. O'Farrell told him, taking a pinch of snuff. "Engrossed in my work, I find the day all too short as it is for what I have to do. So Sir Alvary has done the proper thing, has he? I am a little nonplused, but still very gratified."

"Well, in a manner of speaking. Negotiations are still under way. But we'll be showing it here from tomorrow on, and we wanted you of all people to see it privately first."

You of all people, eh? thought Mr. O'Farrell contentedly, and, taking his leave with a few more nicely chosen phrases, he tripped away with elastic tread, passing the "Cabra Allotments" without so much as a glance. He did not stop again until he came to Grafton Street, where he bought an avocado pear and a bundle of early asparagus.

Mr. Seán O'Hara sat alone in his fine new residence in Leeson Park, smiling contentedly. He was smiling to think how simple the practical arrangements of life became once a man really put his intelligence on them. It was only last night, at quite a late hour, that Michael Nolan had persuaded him he must find an address; had declared that for a man of his coming position to be living anyhow here and there was not to be thought of. For once O'Hara had accepted advice and behaved in a calm and rational way. He had called on a house agent first thing in the morning and had fallen in love with the first property he saw, the upper half of a house in this respectable neighborhood, with a good view of the Protestant church. He had expressed a desire to move in at once, leaving the agent to take up his reference and conclude the formalities in his own good time. Tomorrow he would visit the auction rooms and acquire the necessary furniture; for the moment he sat on the bare boards, leaning his back against the wall, with a dozen and a half of stout drawn up beside him, smiling dreamily into space as he waited for his friend and impresario.

Twilight fell, and then darkness. Something would have delayed Michael, but he was too happy to mind it. It was a grand thing to sit on your own floor under your own ceiling, drinking your stout at home like a gentleman instead of swilling it in some noisy bar. The electric current had not yet been turned on, and the only light there was came from a lamp in the street below, across which the boughs of a tree waved to and fro and made charming patterns on the wall. Seán dreamed of how this room would look when he had it finished. It would have to be Louis XV entirely, he decided, with crimson velvet curtains and a carpet that was soft and rich. There would be one chandelier at least.

Half the bottles were empty when at long last there came a knock on the door. Seán hurried off to answer it, but, accustomed to Michael's basement flat, he commenced to walk up a flight of stairs that in fact led down, and landed in a heap at the bottom. This had the effect of completely spoiling his mood. It had been his intention to receive Michael with a lordly wave of the arm and a "Welcome to Castle O'Hara!" or some such felicitous phrase, but now he flung open the front door and observed in a truculent voice, "And what happened to *you?*"

It was not Michael who stood there at all, but the house agent, whose demeanor was hardly less truculent than Seán's.

"You weren't there when I called earlier," he said nastily. "And my business with you won't wait till the morning. If you want the house, you'll have to pay six months' down in advance."

Seán thought he had never met with such impudence in his life before.

"Rent in advance!" he exclaimed. "Didn't I tell you who I was going to be?"

"Ah, you did," the agent assented.

"And who my reference was?"

"That's just it," snapped the agent, firing up immediately. "You said he was the proprietor of the Grafton Lounge."

"I said no such a thing. I am amazed," cried Seán, "that you should twist my words, my truthful words, in that kind of way. I said he was Mr. Michael Nolan *of* the Grafton Lounge. And I was right to say it. It's where you'll mostly find him."

He made as if to close the door.

The agent introduced the toe of his boot into the crack, and pushed the door in again. He was the sort of sly, foxy, acute little fellow that make artists and thinkers despair of humanity. From the very sit of his hat it was clear that his mind ran on material subjects all day long.

"Now, please!" he said sharply.

With Louis XV and the chandelier at stake, Seán prudently mastered his indignation and attempted to reason instead. "I haven't it on me just now," he said in a low, pleading voice. "Do I look like a man who would carry six months' rent in his pocket?"

"You do not," agreed the agent with a disparaging look at his baggy trousers.

This look was too much for Seán altogether. He could never bear to be judged on externals. It was

what he was, he always insisted, and not what he did
or what he wore that entitled him to the respect of
his fellow men. He had often thrashed this out with
Michael, who shared his point of view absolutely,
finding it both Christian and in keeping with the requirements of plain common sense.

"You low-class, third-rate vulgarian!" he shouted,
dealing the agent a violent box on the ear. The man
staggered back in surprise and pain, missed his
footing at the top of the steps and finished up on his
back in a bed of geraniums. In the houses near by,
windows were hurriedly pushed up and heads poked
out to learn the cause of the commotion; and to these
the agent, supine among the flowers, began to put
his case.

"Battery!" he called out in piteous tones. "False
pretenses to begin with, and battery now!"

"You impugned my integrity!" Seán vociferated.
"You called my honor in question!"

"You, up there! I'll need you as witnesses!" the
agent proceeded.

Every head disappeared as one, and the windows
slammed with a beautiful precision.

"There's Ireland for you!" lamented the plaintiff.

"There's decency, you mean!" riposted Seán. "And
honest human feeling! Viper! Off of my land before
I call the Guards. Contemptible frivoler! Scut!"

The language he employed when the agent
brought a Guard to the scene was such that, in the
subsequent proceedings in Court, it had to be written
down; and to underline his meaning he punched the
Guard in the eye. Brushing his legal adviser aside,
Seán proudly admitted the charges. He believed that
the enormity of the provocation would see him
through. He could not suppose that an Irish Court

would deny to an Irish gentleman the right, the
privilege, the duty, of avenging a slur on his name.
So full of noble wrath was he that four previous appearances in Court, due to jousts of a similar nature,
escaped his memory. It was with real amazement and
grief that he heard himself being ordered to jail for
three months without the alternative of a fine, which
whether he could have paid it or not was surely his
legal entitlement. He left the dock with the fine, con-
temptuous bearing of a Robert Emmet.

"Ah, poor fellow, God help him," Dublin said.

"It was the worry that did it," Dublin opined.

"The television crowd in London can be proud of
their work, all right," growled Dublin.

Mr. Paul O'Farrell read the reports of the matter
with death in his heart.

ten

A week or so after the events described, Mr. Thomas O'Driscoll resolved on drastic action. The absurdity, and the inconvenience, of the position he was in could be endured no longer. While tongues were wagging all over the town about his exploit, and the papers were full of speculation as to its author, he remained unknown and unemployed. He had applied for various jobs that were advertised, suiting his qualifications to their differing requirements in the most intelligent way; but it all came to nothing when he was asked for a reference. He had written courteously and forgivingly to Mr. Pye on the point, but had decided on the whole against using his answer. His money would soon be gone; and with nothing to lose he determined to flout the Organization that treated him so casually and sell his story to the highest bidder.

"One must be fair to oneself," he reflected.

On the whole he thought it best to approach a London paper. That the English Press was pagan, corrupted and materialistic he knew; but it seemed to have plenty of money. He had heard admiring tales of men who had sold it stories for a handsome fee and then, on one pretext or another, collected damages when these stories came out. His mouth had watered at the very idea. He therefore telephoned to the Dublin correspondent of one of the liveliest Sunday papers, explained who he was and asked for a proposal.

The discussion that followed was something of a disappointment.

"Then it wasn't the I.R.A. after all," the journalist commented.

"No; an independent organization. We work with the I.R.A.," Tommy said, "but we are a separate body."

"I never heard of any such thing."

"You wouldn't, of course. And I am not allowed to reveal any details of it now. What I offer you is my personal story of how I went to London and recovered the picture. Provided the money is right," he added.

"It's a story and no mistake," the man said doubtfully. "But I'd have to consult the Editorial. The trouble is, we've always taken the line that it was the I.R.A. We've had special articles denouncing them in our home editions, and sympathetic appraisals of patriotic endeavor, however misguided, in our Irish ones. The Editor won't like this at all."

"What's in a name?" Tommy asked with hauteur. "Aren't we every bit as good?"

"I dare say, but that's not how newspapers work," the man said patiently. "Once they decide a thing is so, it is so, as far as they are concerned. But here's what I suggest. I'll put a check for five pounds in the post to you right away, for the option on an exclusive. Then I'll talk to London and see what they say. It may take a little time."

"Very well, so, but I can't wait forever."

Tommy put the receiver down and sat thinking things over. The more he thought, the more it seemed to him that he was a wronged man. He had brushed the Press of his dear native land aside and given the preference to the foreigner; the least he had expected in return was an immediate bid running into three, or possibly four, figures. All he had got was a beggarly five pounds to shut his gob while the story grew cold. Were all English newspapers as tricky as this? His latent suspicions of the whole race promptly came to life. He had always heard they were sharp as foxes, behind those simple looks they had.

Suddenly a brilliant notion struck him. If, as he suspected, he was being done in the eye, the best plan was to find it out at once. It was a matter of self-preservation. He telephoned to the British Embassy for the names and numbers of all the correspondents of English Sunday papers, saying that he wished to hold a Press conference. He was amazed at the bold and masterful way he spoke down the wire. Then he rang the journalists up in turn and put his proposal to each. To his chagrin, they replied in a monotonously similar fashion. Every one of them had, for this reason or that, to consult their employers before they made an offer; and all of them promised him five pounds down for an exclusive option, except one who suggested three.

"Three pounds!" cried the goaded patriot. "The others all gave me five!"

"What others?"

Tommy recovered himself at once. "In the past when I had a good story I always got five for the option," he said earnestly. "I am by no means a beginner."

"Well, if you know where to get five, don't let me stop you."

"No, no; I'll take the three. I wanted your paper to have this; that's why I rang you first."

How matter-of-fact and unimpressed they all did sound, Tommy thought with irritation. You'd imagine it was a flower show he was reporting. He supposed the profession must make them callous and dull. But when all the negotiating was over he grew more cheerful. It was the old story of the bird in the hand. Eight fives were forty, plus three, forty-three. He had never had forty-three pounds in his life before, or anything like it. All the rest of the day he was on tenterhooks lest they should change their minds, or perhaps had merely been codding him all along. That night he barely closed an eye. But the Pressmen kept their word and the checks arrived together by the first post of the morning, and as Tommy opened them one by one his heart grew warm within him and it seemed as if the world had burst into song. He spread them out over his bed and stroked them lovingly, crooning gentle, foolish words to them as if they had been children or animals.

"You've saved my life," he whispered over and over again.

Far away he heard the shriek of the telephone bell and Mrs. Barry hurling imprecations at it.

"I'll answer," came in Felix's laughing voice.

"I should let it ring. It'll get tired presently. Anyhow, I am out."

Peadar interrupted himself in the act of sawing a lot to ejaculate, "God help us!" to the world at large. He was smarting under a recent allegation of untruthfulness made by his employer, and missed no opportunity of evening things up a little.

"It's for you, Tommy," Felix called up the stairs.

Tommy thrust his checks under the pillow and ran down to where—surrounded by gardening tools, bags of seed, coils of wire and fishing tackle—the telephone had its niche. A voice from the end of the wire announced that its Editor would buy the story and would pay him fifty pounds for it.

"Which one are you?" he asked in his foolish excitement.

"Which one am I?"

"I mean, which story do you mean?" Tommy hurriedly said, while a warm blush spread over his cheek. Really, you needed your wits about you for dealing with the Press. "I had another about . . . about an Irish horse for the Derby," he said with a poor attempt at airiness, "but it'll be the picture you're thinking of, I suppose. You'd . . . you'd hardly pay fifty pounds for the one about a horse, I imagine," he said reasonably. "It wouldn't be economic at all. Extravagance, really. Right you are. I'll take it."

He was much too flummoxed to bargain. There was a pause from the end of the wire, and then the voice said, "I hope this is on the level."

"Of course it is," cried Tommy with real indignation.

"How do I check your story?"

"You must take my word for it," Tommy told him frostily.

"Very well. In that case, though, I'll have to print it as a straight personal interview, in your own words. That suit you?"

"Certainly."

When at last the journalist had done with him, Tommy felt as if he had been turned inside out. In particular he resented the fellow's way of putting his questions a second time and pouncing on any little discrepancy that arose in the answers. It was like Russia, or lawyers; an ingrained suspicion appeared to characterize this whole fraternity.

"You understand, don't you, that none of this material can be offered to anyone else until after Sunday?"

There he went again!

"Please come to this office at two, to sign the interview and have your photograph taken."

From his manner of speaking you would think he had bought Tommy body and soul. The young patriot acquiesced, however, for he loved to be photographed and he hoped to collect his fifty pounds. The total bag now stood at ninety-three, far short of his anticipations, but still good going. Tommy regretted having to disappoint the others, but an option was an option; if all parties were not equally free to opt, in his opinion, it was a pretty bad business. That ready sixth sense of his, nevertheless, warned him to cash his checks without delay, and this would mean opening a bank account, as he had never possessed such a thing.

Having passed a comb through his red curls and put on his tie in order to impress the Bank, he set out on his expedition with a light heart. Already he began to wonder if his main talent were not, after all, for business. But just as he was closing the front door, an individual with a camera and flash-lamp, and an air of having slept in his clothes, inquired if by any chance he were Thomas O'Driscoll. The individual seemed a little nonplused by Tommy's affirmative.

"What in the world can you have been up to?" he asked, eyeing the young man with mingled doubt and respect. "I've orders from five London papers to get your picture. My phone never stopped ringing since eight this morning."

"I'm sorry, but I cannot permit it," Tommy replied. "I have disposed of the option."

"But they were most insistent!" the man cried, staring at him. "They said you'd know all about it. They made me promise to get the pictures first thing. They have to post them this evening. I dropped another assignment to get here. I can't afford this!" he wailed. The bony tip of his nose moved agitatedly up and down as he talked, adding pathos to his remarks.

"Is that right?" asked Tommy in commiseration.

"This is the second time I was let down in a week! I'm a poor man!"

"Oh, that's desperate," mumbled Tommy.

"Wife and chiselers!"

"Oh, Lord. How many?"

"Nine. Ten on Tuesday, D.V." All this was the purest invention, but the photographer had accurately sized up his man.

"Ah, no! Ah, no!" A lump came into Tommy's throat at the thought of all those chiselers to be fed. His imagination began to race, as it always would at the drop of a hat. It sped easily on to the end of act two, where the little ones cried bitterly in their tiny, cheerless room as implacable men bore the furniture away; and his own eyes grew moist. "Take your old pictures, so," he said. "I'll be ruined, but I can't see you stuck."

"Just let me take them, there's the great lad," the man said eagerly. "You can smooth it over with the papers afterwards. They'll have to pay me. I was to get five pictures, and that is all I need know."

Despite a few misgivings as to the correctness of the procedure, Tommy thoroughly enjoyed the half-hour that followed. The photographer became a new man the minute his point was gained, and showed himself as both imaginative and businesslike. First he inquired in a methodical way as to the story he was to illustrate, and on learning who Tommy was and what he had undergone for Ireland, sang his praises until the hero was covered in happy confusion. Then he asked to see the house, as shots were always more natural in the subject's own surroundings. On the stairs they passed Mrs. Barry, attired in a flowing green mantle with a circlet of gold riding her brow. She was about to begin some sketches for a new edition of Lady Gregory and proposed to use herself as a model; also, it helped her to feel the text.

"Is that lady your mother?" he whispered with the air of a man who never misses a trick.

"No; my Landlord."

"A pity."

When they reached the attic the photographer glanced about him keenly and yet in a matter-of-fact sort of way, as if polar bears and warming pans were the stuff of everyday life. Then he sank onto the bed, where he sat in deep meditation with a forefinger pressed to his temple. At last he sprang up and opened the window.

"Right. The Dreamer, to begin with," he said

briskly. "Just sit by that, will you, and look wistfully over the blue hills of your native land."

After the Dreamer came the Son of the People, when Tommy had to pretend to fry a sausage in his pan. This was followed by Divine Discontent, with Tommy full-length on the bed in his shirt sleeves, haggardly staring upwards.

"You'd better be smoking for this one," the artist said, pushing a damp yellow stub into the model's hand.

"I don't smoke, thank you."

"Doesn't matter. It looks more discontented."

It was astonishing how much creative thought the fellow packed into so short a time. For Resolution he wanted Tommy to strip to the waist, but the young man, concerned for his narrow white shoulders, objected to this on the grounds of modesty. As an alternative he offered to undo a button or so of his shirt and plunge his hand into his bosom; but the photographer shook his head.

"Corny," he said. "All right, we'll skip Resolution and try the religious angle. Got your rosary? Then twist it in your fine, nervous fingers and shut your eyes. That's the boyo. Hold it! Faith of my Fathers.

"That'll do for the MacGregor and Epstein group," he added, sliding the plate away with an approving little pat. "They're nuts on simple faith."

The final shot was of the Dream Come True, in which Tommy sat reading an account of hs exploit in the paper, with a wonderful mixture of humility and triumph on his face. The photographer was laughing so much he could hardly take it.

"God, you were born to this," he cried. "Oughtn't you to be on the stage? Honest, you'd make your fortune there."

When the man took his leave Tommy stayed behind in the room, smiling appreciatively at himself in the looking glass. He could not but feel that a milestone was reached in his career. With a single leap he had joined the ranks of the celebrated, the film stars and politicians and bishops who got their names in the papers. He was a man with whom henceforward MacGregor and Epstein would have to reckon. What took his breath away was the rapid, simple manner in which it had all come about. Only three days ago he had been penniless, obscure, a creature of no account, facing an empty future. Now he had forty-three pounds in his pocket, with another fifty to come, and the world was about to ring with his name. The excitement and pleasure of it drove all other things, Ireland included, out of his head.

"There's plenty of room at the top, me lad," he murmured, dealing himself a conspiratorial wink in the glass.

Then all at once he remembered, with a stab of pain, that the pictures could never be used, owing to this detrimental agreement he had been bamboozled into making. He had pledged himself, in his youth and inexperience, to a single organ. But could they perhaps be printed by themselves, with a note underneath to say that the full account was to be found in such and such a paper? He doubted that English editors were capable of so much *esprit de corps*. Rather than raise the circulation of a colleague, even once, they would suppress material of interest and importance to the public as a whole. The spirit that moved them was a mean and commercial one; they were irresponsible.

While he sat musing in this vein, Felix called him to the telephone once more.

"You're in demand this morning, dear warrior," he said as Tommy ran down the stairs. "Are the Press coming up to scratch?" For, needless to say, Tommy had not embarked on so bold a course without consulting his knowledgeable friend. "They're nibbling, all right," he replied with a mysterious nod.

"Then hook, land and gaff without delay. I've an invitation for us both that is not to be missed."

The first words that came over the wire sent Tommy's active mind on a new tack altogether.

"Mr. O'Driscoll? Elwes here. Sorry I was so skinny over the option money," the voice began. "You never can tell with these things. But the Editor's keen as mustard, and he is offering sixty guineas."

Sixty guineas! the other fellow had diddled him nicely, then. You needed an agent, really, in dealing with that class of shark. Oh, but Tommy O'Driscoll was able for him, just the same. He'd whip the superior smile off his mug!

"I'll take it, Mr. Elwes," he said, in cool, businesslike tones. "You'll want just a personal interview in my own words, I imagine."

"That's the ticket. By the way, did Sweeney get out to you for the photograph?"

"He did. He's after leaving this minute."

"Fine. Well, fire away. I'm listening."

When Tommy had finished his interview and had promised to call in later to sign it, his first impulse was to ring up that other dirty cheat and tell him the deal was off. But then a thought came into his head that really made his flesh creep. He had been diddled once; suppose he were being diddled again? For Tommy believed that such things as his story had an absolute, fixed market price, like a motorcar or a tin of tomatoes. He himself had imagined it variously between five hundred pounds and a thousand. The wisest plan, he thought, was to wait for a bit and see. As the papers got on to him one by one, he would accept the offers that were better and reject those that were worse. But in the case of the latter—mercy, the complication!—there was bound to be a fuss about the option money and he had not yet cashed the checks. He worried these facts in his mind until at last, dazzling in its simplicity, the perfect solution presented itself. He would accept all offers good or bad, give the story out all around, cash the checks and then ring the unsuccessful candidates up on Saturday morning to say that the deal was off.

"That'll leave them with nothing to kick at," he argued in his clear-sighted way.

The plan, as simple well-laid plans are apt to do, went smoothly into execution. Tommy sat down by the telephone with a pencil and paper, and waited. One by one the correspondents rang him up and one by one they received a full report. The story grew richer and richer with the steady practice in telling it, and the Pressmen were all delighted. Only in the case of the very last one was there a recrudescence of the suspicion that Tommy found so deplorable.

"Your line's very busy this morning."

"It isn't my line. This is a large house, full of writers and artists."

"You know what 'exclusive' means, don't you?"

"I wasn't born yesterday. But if you don't trust me . . ."

"All right, all right. Of course you wouldn't offer the story elsewhere. But I don't want you even to give out that there is one. We're going to splash it as a scoop."

You are in me eye, thought Tommy. This was another fifty-pounder. "I'll not breathe a word," he said, crossing his fingers as he spoke in order to square his conscience.

He had every reason to feel content with the morning's work. The highest bid had been for seventy-five guineas, and this in a way was galling. Yet a concrete hundred and twenty-one pounds and fifteen shillings were not to be despised; and unlimited possibilities in follow-ups, memoirs, even it might be a serialized biography, appeared to lie ahead. One of the Irish papers had just begun, for the twentieth time at least, a series on the heroes of 1916, and at that rate, Tommy concluded, he should be in the money for years to come.

Mr. Horniman was fairly dancing with impatience when at last Tommy crawled from the glory-hole, shaking the cobwebs out of his hair.

"I thought you'd never come to the end of your garrulous reminiscence," he cried. "Hurry up and put your things together, like a dear boy. We're going to spend a few days with Topsy."

Tommy had become used by now to the caprices of the mercurial Felix and as a rule greatly enjoyed them.

"Who's Topsy, at all?" he asked, smiling.

"Impossible to describe her," Felix said. "Lady Mary Butterwind, English, rich, dotty, is the best I can do. The rest you must fill in from observation."

"Oh, I couldn't stay with a lady like that!" Tommy exclaimed in horror. "I haven't the clothes for it. I'd only shame you. You'd wish you never brought me."

For some reason Felix was much amused by the objection.

"Clothes!" he chuckled. "Wait and see. Clothes!"

"I haven't a suitcase! I haven't a sponge-bag! My

pajamas are torn!" continued the panic-stricken hero.
"There'd be a butler, I suppose?" he demanded in
hollow tones, as if with a butler the humiliation
would be complete.

Felix pulled himself together and looked at the
troubled young man with affectionate sympathy.
"What did Uncle ever take you to, that you didn't
enjoy?" he inquired. "Uncle will rummage about in
his simple effects and see what he can spare. Then
you trustfully slip your warm little hand into Uncle's
great big strong one, and go with him."

He made equally light of the other difficulties that
Tommy poured out to him in a muddled stream.
There was no need to open a bank account for the
moment; they would go to Felix's tailor and blarney
him into cashing the checks. "I owe him so much, he
can hardly refuse," Felix said.

The Daimler waited at the door. They would have
a bite of lunch at the Club, after which Felix would
drive him to his various appointments; and then they
would take the road, reaching Topsy's place in the
west in good time for dinner. As Tommy listened, he
began to feel that the idea was really an excellent one
after all. A new life was opening before him, and it
seemed only right that he should accustom himself to
a new kind of society. The feeling was strengthened
when Felix led him into his room and pulled from
under the bed a handsome pigskin bag.

"Now, what color pajamas?" he asked, opening a
drawer. "Not the scarlet, perhaps, with that poll of
yours. How about this attractive little line in king-
fisher blue?"

"I've some most important telephone calls to make
on Saturday, though," Tommy said, as he hungrily
watched him. He had never seen so many pairs of

pajamas before in his life, all made of silk and in the wildest colors; and he resolved to lose no time in acquiring some of his own.

"Topsy has a telephone," Felix assured him. "We won't cut you off from the great world completely."

It was a beautiful silvery-gold noontime of the early summer. The meadows each side of the road to Dublin were gay with buttercups and daisies, and in the gardens the may and laburnum were at the peak of their flowering. As Tommy sat beside Felix, listening to the purr of the motor and looking at the showers of blossom that tumbled over the walls, he gave himself up to the pleasure of the expedition. He was no longer appalled by the prospect of a butler. On the contrary, he saw himself as making an immediate conquest of everyone, high and low, in Lady Mary's establishment. The noblewoman herself, he assumed, would be so taken with Felix's shy and unworldly, though brilliant, friend that she would not wish to part with him. She might well desire his plays to be written under her roof. He was just helping himself to a peach from a silver bowl with one hand while he polished up an epigram with the other, when he noticed that Felix was quietly laughing.

"Dreaming again!" Felix remarked. "What I've been saying to you, in case you are interested, is that I'm jolly glad to be out of Dublin this week end."

"Me too," said Tommy with a happy sigh.

"Ah, but you haven't my problems to face," Felix told him. "A frightful hag has just arrived, *sur ma piste,* at the Shelbourne Hotel. Six foot two in her stocking'd feet and with one of those huge, red, county faces. She means to marry me and, horrible to say, she has that crazy aunt of mine on her side. How she found out I was here, I can't hope to discover.

The tenacity! It's no bad idea to go to earth for a day or two."

"Sure, you couldn't be married," observed Tommy in a man-of-the-world kind of way. "You're much too young!"

"I shall never see thirty again, dear child."

"I know. Time enough to be thinking of marriage in fifteen years. A man shouldn't rush into that sort of business."

"My sentiments exactly. I never before met such an old head on young shoulders," Felix approved. "But women are terrifying, once they make up their minds. It's been a damned close-run thing once or twice."

"And the woman's a fright, you say?"

"A monster. My aunt says she would have a steadying influence. And while, of course, dear Auntie is above such things, she's got a million pounds."

"A million pounds!" bawled Tommy, sitting up straight. "A million pounds, and you won't have her!" The frivolous attitude that Felix brought to serious matters was an eternal vexation to him.

"Not if she had two."

"She could have two heads, for me, if she liked!"

"And you could make them comfortably from the one she has, with something to spare."

Tommy was shocked to hear a millionairess described with such levity. It struck him, too, and not for the first time, that there was something impious in such indifference to the favors of Heaven. Felix, of course, was rich, while he had nothing to offer but a name, and he wouldn't have that until Sunday; but the mere thought of the lady's presence in Dublin sent the blood coursing faster in his veins.

"What's this, her name is?" he asked in a reverent tone.

"Prunella Gibbing."

"And staying at the Shelbourne?"

"That's right, the lucky people. Remind me to put on my false mustache before we reach the Green."

"I hope they look after her," Tommy sighed. He withdrew into the interior once more. Give me the Shelbourne Hotel, he said authoritatively to someone. Hallo? Miss Prunella Gibbing, please. Miss Gibbing? Miss Gibbing, you won't know me from Adam . . . no. Ye'll not know me from a hole in the wall, of coorse, but Oi'm wondherin' have ye all ye need to make your stay wid us a pleasant wan. . . . How very strange that you should ask! I find myself completely at a loose end. Ye'd never come out to the fillums with a fellow ye didn't know? Oh, I could hardly . . . Ah, come on now, girleen! Sure, there's no harm in me. . . . Well, since you're so very kind . . . A bit far-fetched, perhaps? Even a little uncalled-for? He thought on the whole it was, and sighed again.

The afternoon went by in the easy way that afternoons had when Felix was in charge of affairs. With a delightful wad of notes in his inner pocket, Tommy ordered his luncheon at the Club as confidently as if he had three different things for the one meal every day of his life; and in fact he was rather getting into the way of it nowadays. When they could eat no more, Felix beckoned to the waiter.

"I want a pie, a pound of Limerick ham in slices, a small Stilton, three loaves, any amount of butter and half a dozen of the claret," he said. "Put them up with some cutlery and a corkscrew, there's a good fellow."

"You're not still hungry?" Tommy cried. He himself could hardly move in his chair.

Felix gave a mysterious chuckle. "Not at the moment," he said. "Well, Thomas O'Driscoll, scourge of
the Saxon, it is ten minutes to two. Your duties to the
public claim you. We'll call for the iron rations later.
Come on; no hanging back, if you please. You stand
at last on the threshold of fame."

Tommy wiped his face with a napkin and obediently followed him out to the car.

eleven

The appearance of Lady Mary's mansion was all and
more than Tommy had expected. The country round
about was hilly, and the way ran up and down slope
after slope until, from the summit of one higher than
the rest, the great house could be seen a mile or two
off, perched on another with a gentle valley rolling in
between. In this valley little groups of sheep browsed
here and there as if posed for an engraving, and the
early haycocks threw long shadows in the evening
sun; sharp against the sky in the distance were the
pointed mountains, blue at the peak, tawny below.
Mighty trees fringed the back and sides of the house
itself; vast wrought-iron gates barred the way to a
long avenue, lined with more trees, which led to the
front door; and on either side of the avenue there
stretched away gardens—rose gardens, Italian gardens, water gardens—with follies, summerhouses,
pools, pergolas and Grecian urns, where bent figures

could be seen toiling despite the lateness of the hour.

All through the long drive from Dublin, Tommy had been impatiently looking forward to this moment; but now that it had come, his fears returned at once, taking the form of a sharp hostility to what he saw. It seemed to him that the place breathed out an air of wealth and privilege and insolence, and, he remembered, it was in English hands. What was the use of chasing the English out if they came back armed with their checkbooks, and established themselves again with the connivance of the native Government? Was it for this his fathers had fought and died? It was fellows like himself, whose forebears sweated and starved to build these arrogant strongholds, that should be living here. Now a woman hurried out of the lodge to open the gates for them, and into her respectful greeting Tommy read the enslavement, the mental bondage, of his country. Halfway up the drive a young man, apparently in the last stage of exhaustion, was trying to break a stone with a crowbar; and as Tommy saw the poor arms attempt feebly to raise the tool so much too heavy for them, and heard the groan that burst from the dry lips, he felt that by simply coming here as a guest he was a traitor to his people.

Felix, however, stopped the motorcar at once, with a merry shout.

"Freddie, dear soul!"

The serf looked languidly up and straightened his back. "Ah, Felix, that you? Heard you were coming," he mumbled. A febrile light shone in his eyes. "Anything to eat or drink in that bus?" he inquired with pitiful eagerness. "I've been here since noon. A glass of barley water on arrival, and two sardines on toast for luncheon. How d'ye do," he said with a weary nod to Tommy.

"Forgive me. Mr. Davenport, Mr. O'Driscoll. Yes, we have a variety of little snacks on board. But we must husband our resources. I didn't know there was to be a party, and I've brought no more than what will fairly keep life in the two of us. And it's nearly dinnertime."

"Dinner!" said Mr. Davenport with a bitterness dreadful to hear. "She's out for dinner. You know what that means."

Mr. Horniman did know, apparently, for his face all at once grew pensive. Without another word he opened the hamper supplied by the Club and began cutting thick slices of bread and butter. Mr. Davenport snatched them from him the instant they were ready and crammed them in beastly fashion into his mouth. He seemed indifferent to what figure he might be cutting, and made a curious growling noise as he chewed. When Felix unwrapped the Limerick ham, he leaned over and made a snatch at it.

"Steady, old dear, you'll do yourself harm," Felix cautioned, whisking it away. "And we are here for three days. Now try that to go on with. Don't glare in that lustful way at the bottles, for I'm not going to broach them yet. Do you know whom we have with us this evening?" He broke off to administer a sharp slap to Mr. Davenport's hand as it furtively moved toward the pie. "O'Driscoll, hero of the Morgan Gallery raid. He's just broken his long, dignified silence and given the story to the Press."

"More work for me on Monday," Freddie lamented, still eating away for dear life. "What a week this has been! Stolen pictures. Mayor of Mul-

lingar demands apology from the B.B.C. Sea gulls
again, of course. Are you really not going to give me
a drink, Felix?" he asked in a weeping voice.

"No," Felix replied. "I was nicely brought up and
I haven't yet greeted my hostess. You'd better come
to the house and have one there."

"Can't. I am to finish these stones before dinner.
Topsy invited me down for a rest," he added with his
awful laugh.

"Poor soul," Felix said to the bewildered Tommy
as they drove on up the avenue. "He must have forgotten Topsy's little ways. She believes that her
guests should earn their keep, you know, on the Sal-
vation Army principle."

The great front door swung open as Felix stopped
the engine, and an old woman dressed in black and
with a forbidding expression on her face stood on the
threshold. A barefoot boy in ragged trousers ran
down the steps and began collecting the luggage.

"Late as usual, Master Felix," the old woman observed.

Felix tore up and folded her in a loving embrace.
"Sour as ever, Mifflin," he replied. "And it's only an
hour or two."

"Three," Mifflin said. "Her ladyship was obliged
to go and dress for dinner, without waiting for you.
But as you've come from Dublin, you are each to have
one glass of sherry. Good evening, sir," she said
severely, noticing Tommy, and led them through the
hall to the drawing room.

Tommy had never been in a room of this size before, and it reminded him very much of the films.
There were six huge windows in it, hung with heavy
curtains of yellow satin. The carpet was so deep and
soft that it was like walking over a bed. The paper on

the wall was striped with gold. Whichever way he turned his wondering eyes, he saw sofas and chairs with curly legs and covered with silk brocade. There were a great many portraits of old-fashioned people and pictures of horses and dogs, and right in the middle of the ceiling hung a great glittering chandelier, which he supposed was made of diamonds. Immediately below this was a table on which stood a tray with two small glasses and a decanter.

"Now then," said Mifflin. With a practiced hand she poured a few drops of the brackish liquid into each glass, and firmly replacing the stopper, carried it out of the room.

"Come, let us make beasts of ourselves," said Felix, handing a glass to his friend and taking a sip from the other. At once his mouth contracted painfully, as if he had bitten a green apple. "It's two years since I had Topsy's sherry," he remarked. "Strange how the mind forgets."

"I think it is very nice," Tommy said in a small, hushed voice.

"Bless you. Oh! By the way, before she comes down," Felix began hurriedly, "there's one little thing you should know . . ."

He was too late, for the door opened to admit their hostess, who advanced toward them with the leisured dignity of a cardinal entering his cathedral. Lady Mary was the well-born relict of an industrialist who proved after his death to have several million pounds less than had been believed; and she was fond of declaring that she did not know which way to look for her daily bread. Immediately after the war she had removed to Ireland to escape the crushing burdens, financial and spiritual, of week-end visits from her relations. She was a tall, erect old lady, with white hair

arranged in the style of a bird's nest and faded blue
eyes in which vagueness and acuteness struggled for
supremacy; and her evening gown, which she had
made herself on the previous day from an old muslin
curtain, was of a grubby yellow, hemmed with a
greenish thread. An emerald necklace hung around
her throat and her hands were loaded with rings that
flashed and sparkled; and to complete the ensemble
she had stuck a pink paper rose in her hair.

"Dear boy! How good of you to come all this way
to see an old woman," she began in a tone that did
not fit the words. "And this is General O'Driscoll's
son. I am delighted to see you, dear. Any son of the
General's is welcome in my house. What a very plain
boy!" she soliloquized.

"No, Topsy. Not that O'Driscoll."

"Then which, Felix? That is the only O'Driscoll I
know."

"He is a friend of my own, called O'Driscoll."

"I see," was Her Ladyship's frigid comment.
"Turning the place into an hotel," she noted. "I have
got to dine with our Rector, Felix. On Saturday the
Church fete is to be held in my grounds, when I am
sure you will both want to make yourselves useful.
Mifflin gave you sherry, I see. Such an expense.
What is your name, dear?" she inquired of Tommy.

"O'Driscoll, ma'am."

"Ah, to be sure. We've been into that, haven't
we? Why is he running about with you, Felix?"

"Topsy darling, I explained it all to you on the
telephone. This is the young Irish patriot who recovered the painting from the Morgan Gallery."

Lady Mary put up a lorgnette and treated Tommy
to a careful examination. "He had no business to,"
she said. "There is no excuse for theft but hunger. If

a man is hungry we may perhaps forgive him. Tell Mifflin not to leave things about," she instructed herself. "But perhaps he was hungry, Felix?"

"I was starving," Tommy said with a happy intuition.

"There, Felix; you never told me that. You went chattering on about Ireland and patriotism and nonsense of that kind. It made me think there was something fishy about the boy. Now the whole matter is clear," she said, raising the lorgnette again. "A sad story. His father always kept such a good table. You are in the Blue Room, Felix, and Mr. O'Driscoll in Primrose. No smoking in bedrooms and be sure to turn all the lights off when not in use."

With that she left the room at the same unhurried pace as she had entered it.

"Well, that's Topsy," said Felix with the proud air of a showman.

The questions piling up in Tommy's mind now began to pour out.

"Why does she think I am General O'Driscoll's son?"

"She probably doesn't," was Felix's tranquil rejoinder, "but there is a reason for everything she does, and we shall find it out presently."

"Why doesn't she wear a better dress, if she has so much money?"

"Most people as rich as Topsy are a bit peculiar," Felix assured him. "It is only semi-paupers like myself who know how to live. Topsy surpassed herself over my christening. She's one of my godmothers and, a few days after the ceremony, she sent in a bill for her traveling expenses. And never so much as a silver spoon did I get from that day to this; just a card at Christmas, with the middle part missing."

"But she seems to be spending a good deal on the garden?"

"Her one extravagance. And much of the labor is free at that, as you will discover all too soon."

"It's all very different from what I expected." Now Tommy carefully scrutinized the palms of his hands. "Felix," he said, in a humble beseeching voice, "Felix, am I really all that plain?"

"Not a bit of it," Felix promptly answered. "You have what is known as a dear face. And a most charming expression. I was about to warn you of Topsy's habit of thinking aloud, when she came in. It makes enemies for her."

Tommy heaved a fervent little sigh. "You are kind to me," he said.

"Stuff."

Mifflin put her head, with the new embellishment of a snowy cap and streamers, around the door.

"Which of you is going to have the bath, Master Felix? Whichever it is must look sharp. Dinner is in half an hour."

"Oh, can't it wait till bedtime, dearest Miffles?"

"And keep the stove in!" ejaculated the housekeeper. "I dare say."

"Then up with you, my brave Thomas. You are the guest of honor."

Left to himself, Felix wandered across the room and looked out at the distant hills. There came into his mind, with extraordinary vividness, an episode of his childhood in India. It had been his seventh birthday; he had dined with his parents for the occasion and afterwards sat with them on the veranda, with a dish of sweets beside him. All at once they heard a piteous exclamation and, looking around, saw perched on the rail of the veranda a small gray monkey, whose eyes were fixed on the sweets with such an intensity of longing that they all gave a shout of laughter. The monkey flew into a passion, scolding them and clapping his little paws in rage, until the *syce* came and drove him, still muttering and looking back at the sweets in anguish, out of the compound. What on earth had put this into his head, he wondered, after so many years in which he had barely thought of India once?

Now Mr. Davenport stumbled into the room and collapsed on the nearest chair, rubbing his swollen hands with a look of tender self-pity. "The boss has gone, so I knocked off," he said exhaustedly. "While I've got you alone, Felix, what are you about with that fellow? It's all very entertaining, I dare say, but extremely awkward for me."

"I didn't realize you would be here," Felix replied. "No one need hear of it. Don't start being official with me, I beg."

"I eat Her Majesty's bread," Mr. Davenport reminded him. "And my life is a crucifixion as it is. You caught the merest glimpse of it the day you called. Anonymous letters. Anonymous telephone calls. Anything but anonymous deputations of half-baked students, demonstrating on behalf of Arabs, Cypriots, Egyptians, Irish jailbirds and any pesky blackamoor that takes their fancy. Oh, and the gay whirl of my social round!" he continued on a rising note. "Peasants conferring honorary degrees in the humanities on other peasants. Tea parties at Maynooth. It's more than flesh and blood can bear, Felix; it is indeed. One of these days I shall go berserk. My predecessor is still on the sick-list, after eleven months. He used to lie in bed and sob like a child. And now I'm let in for a week end with your O'Driscoll. If the Ambassador gets to hear of it!"

"What's he like, your Ambassador?" asked Felix sympathetically.

"He's like ambassadors," Mr. Davenport told him, accompanying his words by the peculiar laugh which, with the bald patch on his head and the lines on his face, had been added unto him since Felix saw him last. "And don't pretend that you care. If there's one thing I can't abide, it's this charming insincerity of yours. Had you an Irish grandmother by any chance?" he demanded, while an obsessive glare came into his eyes.

"Now, now! You are growing morbid," Felix soothed him. "But you will be kind to poor little Tommy now we've come? He's such a dear."

"He looks a miserable specimen. Why in Heaven's name have you taken him up?"

"He amuses me," Felix said, in full, and to himself adequate, explanation of the whole story. "More than words can say. And he reminds me of someone, though I can't think whom."

Frederick gave a snort of impatience.

Meanwhile the object of their discussion was becoming more closely acquainted with the marvels of high country life. Mifflin had conducted him upstairs to the Primrose Room, where, on a huge four-poster bed under yellow silk hangings, the pajamas Felix had lent him were already laid out for the night. Without a word she had pushed into his hands a vast yellow towel and, beckoning, had led him away down a long passage through which, despite the sunny stillness of the weather outside, a half-gale appeared to be blowing. She had ushered him into another im-

mense room, with a marble floor, in one corner of
which was a tiny battered bath of antique design.
The half-gale followed them in and made itself
thoroughly at home, while in the rusty pipes that
ringed the walls a similar natural force moaned and
soughed; and as Mifflin turned on the taps a kind of
shudder seemed to run through the whole great
house and a rumble, as of expostulation, came from
regions far below. There followed a pause, during
which Mifflin stood, with folded hands, and scowled
at the bath, and an enormous black spider paced
agitatedly to and fro on the rim as if he were responsible for it all. At last both taps came on to rain,
the drops falling faster and still faster until a tiny
thread of water was pouring from each.

"It's working," Mifflin said with grim satisfaction.
Pointing to a mark that had been scratched on the
enamel about three inches from the bottom, she went
on: "Turn the water off, sir, if you please, when it
reaches that. Otherwise there will be none for the
washing-up. And you will have to make haste." With
that she left the room.

As Tommy sat shivering in his little pool and listening to the querulous plaints of the installations, he
thought that all this was the height of luxury. Only
once or twice in his life had he actually immersed his
body before; his mother was dead against it, believing that it soaked the protective oils out of the
skin and opened the way to consumption, rheuma-
tism and all kinds of other diseases; and his practice
therefore was simply to wash himself all over now
and again, when he felt in the mood. But it seemed to
him that staying in a house like this—where a fellow
like Pye would never get a toe in the door!—brought
its obligations as well as its pleasures; and when at

last, blue with cold, he joined the men downstairs, he had a sense of having undergone a severe but rewarding rite of initiation.

". . . you'll see, the little worm will turn on you: they always do, they can't help it," Mr. Davenport was saying as Tommy came in. Hearing the door he glanced around and hastily got up, while a winning smile spread over his face. "Come and sit down, do," he said expansively. "I am so delighted to make your acquaintance. Forgive me if I was a little offhand in the grounds just now, but I was worn out. Felix has been singing your praises thoroughly."

Rosy with pleasure, the hero mumbled his thanks. The three of them chatted very agreeably together until Mifflin, with a rare defensiveness of manner, came to say that dinner was served and to march them off to the great dining room. On the table here, however, among the gleaming silver and glass and the snowy linen, was something that halted Felix in his tracks.

"Hurry up, Master Felix. We haven't all day," snapped Mifflin as he stood gazing thunderstruck at the collation. "Sit here, if you will, Mr. O'Driscoll; the whole one is for you."

"In all my long and varied experience," said Felix in dire tones, "no one has ever ventured to offer me half a sausage roll before."

"Nice manners, I'm sure," Mifflin retorted with a toss of her head.

"And what is the green thing beside it? A postage stamp?"

"Her ladyship ought to hear you," said Mifflin, firing up. "That's good lettuce, fresh from the garden. Passing remarks! Give over, do, and get on with your meal. There's a nice baked apple to follow, and

Mr. O'Driscoll is to have a glass of whey. Young people nowadays!" she commented to space as she left the room.

Tommy so often went supperless to bed that the enormity of this procedure was lost on him. He was hugely enjoying himself in his splendid surroundings, and had begun to think there must have been some confusion over his birth, that he was really the scion of a noble house who had been swapped with somebody else in his cradle. Without a word, he carefully divided his sausage roll into two equal portions and, leaning over the table, with his knife placed one on Felix's plate and the other on Mr. Davenport's; and this unselfish act he did with such grace as to make a very favorable impression on them both.

"No, no, you good creature," Felix protested, returning the morsel at once. "We needn't starve while we have the pie. But Topsy goes too far; *she goes too far,*" he burst out, with a sudden access of choler that was most unusual in him.

"I've broken my fast, as you know," Mr. Davenport remarked, following the other's example, "but it was a noble thought."

Tommy blushed his vivid scarlet and wound his legs around each other. The housekeeper marched in with three little baked apples, wrinkled and green, and a glass of cloudy liquid on a tray.

"I am gorged, Mifflin," Felix said in a voice that trembled with passion. "I couldn't eat another bite if my life depended on it."

"I too have done remarkably well," said Freddie waspishly.

"Then you'll have it for breakfast, both of you. Such tantrums, my word! But Mr. O'Driscoll must eat his now, and drink his whey. Her ladyship was most particular about it."

As soon as Tommy had complied with these directions, they went upstairs to begin their evening meal. Sitting on the huge four-poster bed under the blue silk canopy, in Felix's room, they spread the good things out and opened a couple of bottles. In the ordinary way as preparations of this kind went forward, Mr. Horniman's face would glow with an almost unearthly happiness; but now he was fretful and touchy and as unlike himself as could be.

"Half a sausage roll!" he reiterated. "It's pathological. It's against nature. It's a monstrous aberration. The smallest chop, the tiniest egg, the dinkiest little banana, *très bien!* I have schooled myself to expect all that in Topsy's house. But to divide a sausage roll in two—can depravity go further? Even to think that a human hand could take a knife and perform a deed like that! Isn't there something terrifying about it?"

"Have some claret, Felix," urged Freddie. "A bad experience makes a good memory. We shall smile at this in days to come."

"Never!" But he consented to take a long, comfortable pull at the wine, and gradually, as time wore on, he recovered something of his normal humor.

Unaccustomed to wine of any sort, Tommy flowered out as an entertainer and raconteur. In quick vivid phrases he told them the story of his life, including a new version of the Morgan Gallery raid and of his final discussion with the Pye. Pye, you hound, that sort of thing breeds communism. Then he volunteered to sing. He sang "The Boys of Wexford" and "The Wearing of the Green," following these up with a jig, executed in faultless native style, with arms and torso stiff as a tree and the dull, wooden look on the face whereby the dancer dissociates himself from the un-Irish abandon of the legs. When he had finished this amid loud applause, Freddie asked permission to recite some verses of an edifying nature that his father had always recited to the family after dinner on Christmas Day.

"The sun, like a Bishop's bottom [he commenced],
Rosy and round and hot,
Shone down on the damned dead niggahs,
The niggahs that we had shot. . . ."

"What is the meaning of this bestial orgy?"

Following a disagreement with the Rector, Topsy had left his house precipitately in the middle of the evening, as her invariable custom was when anything occurred to annoy her. The provocation this time had been considerable. The Rector had been extraordinary. They had discussed the layout of the fete, the side shows, prizes and entertainments in perfect amity; but when Topsy raised the all-important question of how much her share of the takings might appropriately be, he disclosed that he had expected her to lend the Butterwind grounds for nothing! He pleaded that the object of the fete, to raise funds for repairs to the roof of the house in which the curate and his large family were at present being freely rained on, was a worthy one. She retorted that she dared say, but that she was a poor woman herself, a widow whose husband had failed to make adequate provision; that something for nothing was all the cry these days, and in her experience it never answered. The Rector said the arrangement she had in mind was not one he could justify to the Committee nor, he

ventured to point out, was it in her own real interests that he should attempt to do so. Her Ladyship believed she was the best judge of those interests and
desired him to ring for her donkey-cart.

"It's like having pigs to stay," she now reflected.

Both Freddie and Felix were too appalled to
speak. They were struck dumb by their consciousness
of having violated that old and excellent English
tradition whereby all hospitality offered is, *ipso facto,*
perfect. They had infringed that other old and excellent rule of English society which forbids the trans-
gressor to be found out. The outraged faces of parents, nannies and tutors rose before their inward eye
to accuse them, and they looked as guilty and foolish
as two small boys. But Tommy, who had never enjoyed their cramping advantages and was released
by alcohol from all inhibitions of his own, blithely
took charge.

"It's all my fault, Lady Mary," he began with a
radiant smile. "I was hungry."

"Still hungry after dinner!" cried his hostess. "Did
Mifflin give you the whey?"

"She did of course, but there's like an awful, hollow craving inside of me. It comes from the years of
privation. Felix brings boxes of food wherever we go.
I eat like a horse, like a tiger," he said, his imagination completely airborne now. "I was offered a job
in a circus once. At home I keep a cheese the size of a
man to cut away at between meals, but there was no
room for it in the car."

Lady Mary followed this recital with close attention. "I imagine it's a form of disease," she remarked. "Reminds me of old Fatty Bellairs. Ruinous
to have in the house. Still, he has brought his own
tack. I like this poor, ugly child," she enunciated

distinctly. After these words she sank into a reverie while the others waited with bated breath. At last she made as if to speak, but immediately caught herself up; began again, and again thought better of it. She was in that state of painful indecision that may overwhelm even the strongest characters when a choice of peculiar difficulty confronts them. Then she drew a long, deep breath, looking all at once curiously tired and old.

"Mifflin shall boil you an egg for breakfast, dear," she said.

In this manner Thomas O'Driscoll made history again.

twelve

It was the rule for visitors in Topsy's household to rise early. Mifflin herself was invariably out of bed by four o'clock, as the house was a large one for a single old woman to clean and tend and she firmly rejected the services of her lieutenant, a local small girl who was all the inside staff that Her Ladyship's pinched resources could run to. Breakfast was put on the table at seven-thirty and cleared at eight o'clock sharp, when guests unfamiliar with this procedure would find with dismay their half-eaten toast or cup of tea whipped from under their noses without a word. Her ladyship breakfasted in bed and lay then for an hour or so ruminating, until she made her appearance shortly after nine to acquaint each individual under her roof with his tasks for the day.

On this particular morning the work of priority for all hands was to move down to the Rectory everything that had been left at the Hall in readiness for tomorrow's fete. The smaller items, such as fruit, eggs, jam, homemade cakes, homemade sausage rolls curiously similar in form and content to those served the evening before, flowers and jumble, could all be conveyed in Felix's Daimler; but the long trestle tables and the chairs would have to be carried by hand. As the Rectory was over three miles away, they decided to make a start on the heavier items before the sun was fairly up. Canon Mossop saw them stumbling along the road with their burdens while they were yet some distance off, and came hurrying out to learn what was taking place.

"Dear me, this is most unfortunate," he exclaimed when they told him of their mission. "I never dreamed Lady Mary would go so far. There will be a great deal of talk in the village, I fear. Highly undesirable, from the Protestant point of view. And the Rectory garden is not nearly big enough, as Lady Mary knows very well. However, please bring the things along and we'll see what can be done."

"Our little fetes never run smoothly," he continued in a melancholy voice, as they shouldered their cargo again. "The passions aroused last year by the Sweet Pea Competition were truly shocking. A disgrace to a Christian community. And the year before that the tea money was stolen. Not by one of our own, I am thankful to say, and our excellent parish priest saw to it that restitution was made; but it cast a shadow over the day."

The Rectory garden indeed was barely an acre in size, and such open space as it contained was much encumbered with plaster gnomes, toadstools and rabbits.

"Drusilla, my dear, Lady Mary refuses to allow us to hold the fete in her grounds after all," the Canon told his wife; "and these gentlemen have very kindly brought some of the things here, while we consider our next move."

"The old harridan!" was Mrs. Mossop's brisk comment.

"Hush, my dear. These gentlemen are guests of hers."

"Then they had better have something to eat." And she withdrew to the kitchen.

"A quick tongue, but a warm heart." The Canon smiled. "She always keeps a little something in hand for—ha ha!—I was about to say refugees!!—from the Hall. Please make yourselves at home while I do some telephoning."

Mrs. Mossop presently came back with a tray on which was a pitcher of milk, some oat-cakes and a cottage cheese.

"I've seen you before, my lad," she remarked to Felix, busily pouring out and passing. "Are you coming to church on Sunday?"

"I shall do as my hostess desires me."

"Do come if you can; the old boy will be so bucked. One extra voice makes a hell of a difference to the hymns. We have only got twenty-one parishioners now; and Colonel Fowler refuses to sing. And the other parish, that the curate looks after, has thirteen. Ireland is going to pot. Which foot do you dig with, eh?" she asked, darting a keen glance at Tommy.

"I don't dig at all," he told her stiffly, flushing up to his ears.

"Hi! No taking Um over there! Not allowed in this house," Mrs. Mossop cheerily proceeded. "Some of my best friends dig with the other. I always say, we'll get to Heaven just as soon, whichever we dig with. It's the kind of furrow we plow that counts."

Here she discontinued this agricultural theme to urge the offended Tommy, in the kindly voice she used with handicapped children, to drink up his milk. "Think about it, won't you?" she went on to Felix. "Lady Mary comes as a rule, but she has a habit of taking a clock out of her bag in the most ostentatious way when the sermon starts. After exactly ten minutes, she leans back and closes her eyes. Such a rotten example."

Now the Canon returned, all smiles. "People are so kind, my dear," he said joyously. "I explained our little difficulty to Colonel Fowler, and we are to hold the fete there. I trust he does not suppose I was hinting at it. When our young friends have refreshed themselves, perhaps they will add to their already considerable kindness and carry the—ah, *props,* ha ha!—up to his place."

"In all this heat?"

"I fear there is nothing else for it."

"A frightful distance."

"Alas!"

It was twenty minutes after one when the trio, dusty and hot, limped into the dining room of the Hall to find their hostess on the point of rising from the table.

"What an age you've been!" was her greeting. "I was obliged to begin luncheon without you."

"We had to take the things on to Colonel Fowler's."

"Bob Fowler!" exclaimed Topsy with a black look. "Pray, what has Bob Fowler to do with it?"

She was greatly incensed by the new arrangement, having too readily assumed that the fete would have to be held in the Rectory garden and so be a failure. It was her opinion that anyone who crossed her was in need of a sharp lesson, and she never spared herself in the endeavor to see that they got one; and she now hastened away to the telephone to learn what could be saved from the wreckage of her plan. She rang up the Colonel and said that the Rector had misunderstood her and that of course the fete would be held in her grounds as announced. The Colonel, who had fumed and fretted all morning over the inconvenience, replied at once he was damned if it should. Topsy intimated suavely that "her men" would be over in the afternoon to take the equipment away; and the Colonel begged, in that case, they might look out for themselves.

"Everything is all right, my dears," Topsy informed her guests as she re-entered the dining room, noting with approval that their appetites were gone. "You may fetch the things back here as soon as you have finished your meal."

"Why does anyone ever stay with Topsy?" Freddie groaned as they set off down the avenue once more.

"Why does anyone climb Mount Everest?" Felix answered cheerfully. He was in much the best shape of them all; Mr. Davenport's muscles were racked with pain from his ordeal of the evening before, and Tommy was unused to physical exertion of any kind. Yet a new spirit of comradeship had sprung up among the three, born of hardships bravely endured together, welding them into a unit. Frederick began to look on the uncomplaining Tommy with a more appreciative eye, while the hero pitied him as he had never expected to pity an Englishman; and all three felt something of the stern, beautiful fellowship of men at war.

Shortly after turning into the Colonel's gates they heard a sharp report and a cry; and, hastening their

steps, they presently came on the Rector, seated on
the ground and nursing his knee, while the Colonel
stood beside him, fingering a light shotgun and looking sheepish.

"Deuced sorry, I'm sure," he was grunting. "Silly
mistake. The lookout had signaled the enemy, but
the blasted rhododendrons got in me line of vision."

"Oh dear, oh dear," the Canon repined. "It is not
the injury—a mere flesh wound, it will pass, I dare
say; but it is surely a grievous thing that never may
we hold our little parish activities, which ought to
give us all pleasure as well as bring in revenue, without these murderous instincts being unleashed. Lady
Mary informed me of your threats and I hastened
here at once to urge you to reconsider. What sort of
example is this for our Popish neighbors?"

"Damn it, I've said I'm sorry."

"You are sorry, Colonel," said the Canon severely,
"because you were balked of your intended prey. You
have shot me and not one of these kind young men
who have given so much of their time and trouble
to further our plans. That is not true repentance at
all. May I so far trespass on your kindness," he said,
addressing Felix, "as to beg for a, ah, *fireman's
lift?* as far as the house. There my wound may be
dressed and a conveyance procured to carry me home.
And, Colonel, put away that rifle, do," he concluded
peevishly.

"*Rifle!*" But Colonel Fowler lowered the weapon
and, snorting contemptuously, paced ahead toward
the house while Felix and Tommy tottered along in
the rear, bearing the Canon between them.

The Colonel was one of those military gentlemen
whose bite, on the whole, is worse than their bark;
yet he was easily mollified too, and a little bloodshed

was a capital tranquilizer. By the time they reached the front door he had calmed down altogether and begun to play the host. He sent for the vet, the only medical man he would allow on the place, to attend to the Rector's injuries and begged that he might be allowed to pay for repairs to the Rector's trousers. Not only did he make no further objection to Topsy's men removing their gear, but pressed on them a couple of old saddles and some oddments of harness for the jumble sale as well. He insisted on their drinking a pint or so of whiskey and water, and when at last they reeled away in the hot sunlight with their loads, he stood on the steps, affably waving them good-bye.

The events of the afternoon were so much to Topsy's liking that she excused the three from other fatigues for the rest of the day. After the evening meal she proposed a little game of poker, which Felix at once, in an authoritative tone he used but rarely, declined on behalf of them all. Apart from a few asides about the inferior caliber of young men nowadays, she took the refusal well; and sat with them pleasantly chatting and regaling Tommy in particular with anecdotes about the General, whose sporting qualities and fine sense of honor she harped on in a manner that caused Felix to look grave.

"Look out. She's hatching something," he warned his young disciple later as they made their way upstairs. "I know the signs of old. Try not to be left alone with her."

At two-thirty sharp the next day the fete was opened by Lady Mary herself, a striking figure in ragged jodhpurs and with an old green lamp shade doing duty as a hat. It was held in a great paddock behind the kitchen garden, and was attended by crowds of the country people as well as the Rector's own little flock. The Canon himself limped here and there, welcoming them all and smiling broadly as they milled about the stalls; and to encourage trade he moved toward the jumble, with a view to purchasing some trifle of use or beauty for the household. On the way he passed Felix, who waved a book of tickets at him.

"Will you take one, Rector? Only half a crown," he called out.

"Surely that's not a raffle ticket?" the Canon exclaimed. "I gave no authority for anything of that sort. Raffles are illegal, you know, and it is up to us, of all people, to set an example. Pray, how came it into your hands?"

"The chap over there," Felix replied, with a nod of his head at a shaggy young fellow struggling with a saddled horse of wicked appearance some little way off. "His work's cut out for him!"

A mispelled notice beside the horse offered rides on his back for a shilling, with money back and a bonus of a pound for anyone who could stay on for a clear round of the paddock. A number of country lads hovered about the animal, looking sideways at his mad, pale eyes and flattened ears.

"Mug Heffernan again!" said the Rector with a sigh. "And what is being raffled, may I ask?"

"A free ticket for the diocesan pilgrimage to Fatima and Lourdes!"

The Rector started violently, as if he had been shot for the second time. Then, "These people are simply not to be trusted," he said in a low, quivering voice. "Give me that book directly, please. I shall ask the parish priest for an explanation."

As Canon Mossop, badly shaken, proceeded on

his way to the jumble stall, he heard coming from it an altercation unequaled in violence by anything he could remember since the Harvest Festival. Mrs. Bigelow had identified an umbrella put up for sale as her property; she had a clear recollection of lending it to Lady Mary one rainy day after church and she was now cutting up very nasty indeed. Miss Unwin, in charge of the stall and an enemy of Mrs. Bigelow, took the view that all the articles there had originally belonged to someone and that "in times like these" they should pull together for Protestantism and the curate's roof. Mrs. Bigelow would thank Miss Unwin to keep her opinions to herself, and supposed that she was an accomplice in the felony. Miss Unwin thought Mrs. Bigelow had better mind her tongue.

"Ladies, ladies, please!" said the Rector with a familiar sense of exhaustion. He bought the umbrella for five shillings, thus halving at a blow his allocation for the afternoon—how vexed Drusilla would be!—and putting a pot of his favorite rhubarb jam quite out of the question. Then he handed it to the irate Mrs. Bigelow.

"Cast your bread upon the waters," he said with a brave attempt at a smile.

Screams now arose from the direction of the Lucky Dip, in which a small boy was seen to be wedged head downwards.

"O Sacred Heart of Jesus!"

"O Jesus and Mary love him!"

"The little poor lamb! Sure, he'll be killed dead itself!"

The child's relations and friends continued screaming and staring until it occurred to one of them to seize his legs and pull him out; after which they held him upside down between them and shook him furiously to free his lungs of the bran, while his face slowly turned a purplish black.

"How the lower orders do love a commotion!" came in the bell-clear tones of Lady Mary.

Tommy had been placed in charge of the cake and jam stall; and he was displaying powers of salesmanship he had never suspected were his. While as an employee of Kitchen Accessories, Ltd., with his livelihood depending on it, he had been nervous and disparaging of his wares, he now on behalf of a creed and a class he detested pushed them with the fluency and the disregard of fact of a public relations officer. The price of everything was clearly marked, but, disregarding this, he spontaneously held an auction, jerking the figures up by threepences and sixpences with a stream of outrageous patter and silencing opposition with devastating shafts of wit. He was a man inspired, released, fulfilled; and, the very wickedness of his procedure having brought the people on his side, in a short time his stall was swept bare and he stood, flushed and triumphant, looking for new fields to conquer.

"Well, here's a blossoming!" said Felix. The impounding of the raffle tickets had left him nothing to do, and he had been following his little friend's campaign with astonishment and delight.

"Would you ever keep your eye on the money till I get back?" Tommy requested in an offhand yet gracious manner.

"What does the young hero intend doing now?"

"Just to try me luck on the old horse!"

Felix gasped and shot a look of dismay at the animal in question. He was pawing the ground and dementedly rolling his eyes, while Mug, who began to tire of the weight on his arm, thrashed him over the nose with the rein. Mug's pound was as safe as houses: there were no takers at all and the knot of country boys around, who scattered whenever the horse lashed out with his heels, were merely waiting to see Mug knocked down and possibly killed.

"You can't be serious."

"Why wouldn't I be?" Tommy was shivering all over with excitement. "I've ridden better!"

"Don't be such a young idiot," said Felix harshly.

"That's a fine way to talk," cried the incensed Tommy. "Wait till you see me!"

"With a broken neck," Felix went on in the same tone. "Your eyes are bigger than your tummy, my boy. Sorry, but this isn't the moment for make-believe." His affection and terror drove him on to say dreadful things there could be no unsaying. "You are a line-shooting little silly, Thomas O'Driscoll, and you know it as well as I do. You are a crazy, swaggering, inflated little show-off!"

Tommy drew a deep breath. "So that is what you think of me, really," he said in a whisper. Not for a moment had he intended to mount the stallion. He had known that Felix would not allow it, and his idea had been, once the gesture was made, to yield to his friend's entreaties with a show of reluctance, leaving his name for valor to shine with a greater effulgence yet. The appalling, the unbelievable words that Felix had used drove all this from his head, leaving only an icy, terrible resolve. For once in his life he felt not a trace of fear. He would do this thing, he would triumph, he would hear Felix's broken words of remorse and admiration—or he would die. Like a man walking in his sleep, he moved across the turf to the battling Mug and signified, with a brusque gesture, that he was going to mount.

A shout went up from the boys, who at once flung themselves on the animal in the endeavor to hold him still, while Tommy watched them, a sad little smile playing about his lips. His heart was full of that strange love for all mankind that fills our hearts when we hear of a sudden death. Now the horse himself, as if aware that great events were pending, became suddenly quiet and still. Willing hands gave Tommy a leg-up into the saddle, before everyone rushed to safety. For a moment or two the horse stood deep in meditation, wondering which of various attractive courses to pursue, and then, with no trouble at all, sent his rider flying over his head in a graceful parabola and galloped away to the end of the paddock alone.

Tommy lay on his back on the grass amid the ruins of the world, too miserable to speak.

"His back does be broke!" a jubilant cry went up.

"Now what is happening here?" came in the Rector's jaded voice. "Heffernan, do you catch that animal and lead it away at once. Father Meany shall learn of this."

"And me shilling?" asked Mug belligerently. "The fellah owes a shilling, and he's shammin' dead, the way he couldn't pay it."

"Be off," commanded the Rector. "I am always loath to send for the Guards on a charitable occasion, but I shall not hesitate unless you retire. A den of thieves," he murmured, limping away to arbitrate in the fresh dispute now boiling up over the handicaps in the egg-and-spoon race.

Felix knelt on the grass, looking at Tommy's agonized face. "Are you hurt?" he said tenderly.

"No," was the savage reply.

"I was only trying to put you off."

"I see," said the recumbent hero in a sepulchral tone. "I'm sure I ought to be grateful."

"I was afraid of what would happen. You're lucky to be alive. It was a magnificent attempt. You are the bravest chap on earth!" Felix was cooing as sweetly as a woman.

"Blarney!" Tommy slowly got to his feet and, without a glance in Felix's direction, stalked away from the field of disaster toward the house. Looking despondently about him, Felix caught sight of Lady Mary in the act of appropriating a few coins from the bowl on Tommy's stall.

"No, Topsy!" he barked.

"But it's mine, dear, don't you see?" Lady Mary was at her vaguest. "I put it there myself. I am sure I did."

"Nonsense."

Nothing is more offensive than a naked charge of dishonesty; and Lady Mary was visibly nettled. For a moment or two she paused, seemingly inclined to take the matter up, to have it out, to insist on retractions and apologies. But under Felix's calm and steady eye she retired into the mists again and trailed off in the pursuit of Tommy, whom, without apparent effort, she presently overtook.

"I so much dislike the righteous, dear, don't you?" she observed remotely. The full, easy equality of her address had its effect on Tommy's wounded soul; he relaxed a little at once, and she proceeded to follow her advantage up. "Brave child, to mount that stallion. Your father all over again. Come into the library, dear, and I'll show you some pictures of him.

"We'll use the kitchen entrance; it is quicker," she continued. "Mifflin, hang that up or it will spoil," she said, giving her lamp shade to the old woman as they went through the kitchen. "Horribly expensive things, dear, those."

Side by side on the library sofa they turned over the leaves of a number of old picture albums. General O'Driscoll appeared as a bewildering, even a composite, figure: now tall and thin, with flowing mustaches, he glared out with one foot on the leopard he had just shot; then, burly and clean-shaven and arrayed in a deer-stalker, he landed a giant salmon; anon, tricked out in polo kit and a completely new set of features, he received a silver cup from Royalty. Over a heavily bearded gentleman in the full dress of an Admiral of the Fleet, Lady Mary hesitated a little.

"Can that be he?" she wondered. "He was never a sailor, I think.

"A man to be proud of, child," she said, closing the last album with a little sigh. "A man true and tried as steel. He would have died sooner than leave a debt unpaid. He did in fact"—and here a note of lamentation crept into her voice—"die before he could settle with *me*."

"Oh, Lord, is that right?" The General's son was all innocent sympathy. "Did he stick you?"

"No, no no!" laughed Lady Mary. "It was a little debt of honor, child—a game of bridge between friends. I dare say it slipped his memory. It may well have done. It was in 1929."

"Lady Mary," cried Tommy impulsively, rising to the occasion and in fact carried away by it, "I am not a rich man, but if I could . . . if it were within my means at all . . ." The comforting wad of notes in his inner pocket supported him and he would readily at that moment have sacrificed them all.

"Twenty-five shillings, dear," said his hostess with a brisk alacrity far removed from her usual style.

Tommy settled in full immediately, and with a flourish. His mercurial spirits were wonderfully restored by the whole interview; and now to discharge a debt of honor incurred by a General, and at such a reasonable cost to himself, afforded him the liveliest satisfaction. Lady Mary was also well pleased with her work.

"What a nice, funny boy you have brought with you, Felix," she commented later on. "Sometime, not now, you shall tell me who he is."

The rest of the day and the evening passed agreeably for them all. As they sat at their frugal dinner, the accounts given by Felix and Freddie of the latter part of the fete were so hideous, so really blood-curdling, as to cause Lady Mary to laugh out loud. Immediately afterwards she went to bed, exhausted, as she told them, by her efforts earlier on, so that the three young men were able to begin their own meal sooner than they could have expected. Mr. Davenport warmly congratulated Tommy on his gallant try with the horse and would have none of his modest disclaimers. The failure did not matter, he said; what counted was having the guts to try. At any other time Tommy would have seen this remark for the romantic English cod that it was; but now it somehow fitted in with everything else, with staying in a great house, being called "dear" by a titled woman, paying Generals' debts of honor, and altogether with the glamorous absurdity of upper-class life. By the time he went to bed he was in the seventh heaven; and only as he lay in his huge four-poster bed between the deliciously cool linen sheets did a thought strike him so terrible as to make him groan aloud in the darkness.

"O Janey Mack! And I never phoned the papers!"

thirteen

On the Thursday following these events the picture was at last to be on view to the public; and from early in the morning a throng of people betook themselves to it in high good spirits. The Press had been admitted on the previous day, and a photograph of the masterpiece appeared on the front page of every national newspaper. The critics to a man had declared it a work of genius, expatiating on the tactile values, the plastic values, the underlying religious significance and the interesting revolt against naturalism, and urging their readers to stand well back and admire the treatment of the light in relation to the animal's hide. Mr. Paul O'Farrell had given an interview, in which he had dwelt on the "incisive, unmistakable idiom of this Spanish master" and "his glorious, Mediterranean lucidity." Mr. Seán O'Hara, of course, was still in jail.

A lively hum of conversation went up from the

happy art lovers, who were in a mood to be enchanted with everything. The legend written below the picture by some wag—"On Loan from the
Morgan Gallery, London"—was felt by all to be a
master-stroke of tasteful irony. Comment on the work
itself was no less appreciative than informed.

"Isn't it just the most sophisti'cāted thing?" asked
a Minister's wife excitedly of a Senator's wife. "Did
j'ever see anything as sophisti'cāted before? Hallo
there, Mrs. Maguire! So you got here! I'm just after
saying to Mrs. O'Toole, isn't this the most sophisti'-
cāted thing in the world?"

"I hope you are noticing the treatment of the
light in relation to the animal's hide," a sallow young
man with a beard was saying to a girl in a cotton
dress.

"Oh, 'tis gorgeous! Puts me in mind of Jack
Yeats," remarked somebody else to a friend.

"You're right, of course. I'd say the fellow
learned his technique from Jack."

"He was a wee bit older, I imagine."

"Sure, what does that matter?"

Steadily the visitors poured in, including among
them such distinguished persons as a bishop, a judge,
four senators and the managing director of Guinness's
Brewery. There was also a contingent from the Gaelic
League, whose interest, however, was mainly politi-
cal.

"It's a great day for Ireland."

"If they let us keep it!"

"There'll be some fun if they don't."

Soon after twelve o'clock there walked in a woman
and two young men, whose appearance caused a
sudden hush, followed by an excited buzz of voices,
a craning of necks and finally by a spontaneous ova-

tion. Felix had invited Mrs. Barry to accompany himself and the hero of the day to the picture and to a triumphal luncheon afterwards; and the famous features of Tommy O'Driscoll were immediately recognized and saluted. He received the plaudits of the crowd with the most perfect grace imaginable, bowing and smiling his thanks and making little deprecating gestures with his hands, while Mrs. Barry and Felix stood back with the modest demeanor appropriate in friends of the great. They made a striking tableau in which the one peculiarity, the fact that the lady's face was rapidly turning a dangerous purple, went unobserved in the general enthusiasm.

At this moment Tommy was standing on the very peak of human felicity. At last he was enjoying the recognition he had always believed should be his, and enjoying it, moreover, without the preliminary years of struggle and disappointment that greatness has normally to expect. He had returned to Dublin from his rural week end in much trepidation. His oversight in the affair of the newspapers weighed on his mind and his active fancy tormented him with the possibilities of what they might do. But when he reached the capital, to find himself its darling, he soon discovered that this was the very point that gained him the most approval. The simultaneous publication of the story in nine English Sunday papers, each of them drawing attention to the fact that once again it was first with the news, was seen as the crowning touch of a beautiful joke. The divil-may-care young Irishman, who first had braved, single-handed, the might of England and then so wickedly cocked a snook at her Press, fired the local imagination completely; and in no time at all Tommy came to believe that he had intended it all along.

Everybody now wished to make his acquaintance. The local reporters who came besieging the house on the Monday carried him off to town and introduced him to a wide range of notable characters. In the course of the day, as they careered from one bar to the next, he met a bewildering assortment of jockeys, artists, politicians, martyrs who had suffered for Ireland in English jails and all kinds of brilliant people who seemed to have nothing to do but make themselves agreeable to him.

An international footballer took him to supper at Jammet's. Then a famous columnist came up and took him away, as if it had been a Paul Jones, to the pub where the literary stars of Dublin spent their evenings; and here, in company with men whose work had long been known to him, he felt that life could offer nothing more. He was led to a table where, slumped in his chair, there snoozed the greatest living poet; a rising novelist whose books, though banned at home, were said to be the rage in England and America; and a stout, middle-aged man of distinguished appearance who, although at present a civil servant, was one day going to be another James Joyce. His powers so far had not reached fruiting-point; but in the meantime he fleshed his pen and opened the way to his future achievement by critical articles demolishing lesser authors one by one. Tommy's heart beat faster as he heard the well-known name. To be asked to sit down, to be invited to drink, to be accepted by a man who only a month ago had wiped the floor with D. H. Lawrence! He felt that nothing could ever be quite the same again.

The best of all, however, was still to come. Presently a well-dressed man drew up a seat beside

Tommy and began in an undertone to question him as to his ambitions, leanings, experience and present occupation; to all of which the hero answered unfalteringly. The man then said he was in the tourist business and was acting now as a talent scout. There were a number of vacancies in his organization, one of which he thought might appeal to Tommy. This was no less than to assume full charge of the *Come to Lovely Erin* campaign of publicity, whose present incumbent was leaving to take up a post in Manchester. There would be a good salary, generous allowances and the use of a car. If Tommy were interested, he would please to call at the office at ten o'clock on the following morning, when the matter could be discussed more fully.

Long into that night Tommy lay awake, muttering to himself about tides in the affairs of men. He arrived for his interview on the strike of ten, clean and tidy, and resolved to secure the plum if it should be humanly possible. And he could not but feel that he managed things nicely. The eloquence that was vouchsafed to him at certain moments was not withheld on this important occasion; and the description of how he had found Kitchen Accessories, Ltd., teetering toward insolvency, and left it prosperous, expanding and so arranged that a baby could run it, was, in particular, a triumph of disciplined art. Deep in his heart as he rattled on, however, was a nameless fear, to which his interlocutor's final words gave shape.

"Well, that's great," he said. "I'll just have a word with this Mr. Pye of yours, and then we'll meet again."

The pedantry of employers! thought the young man bitterly. Here was that national figure Thomas

O'Driscoll offering his services to an organization that needed them badly, and what must they do but go ferreting about in his dull, dead life that was finished and done with! As he left the office he thought that only a miracle could save him now; and then he thought again, for he was a deeply religious boy, that a miracle might be in the cards. All that was needed was faith; so he had always been told, and he believed it absolutely. Accordingly, he went to the nearest church and prayed to the Little Flower as he had never prayed in his life before. He assured her that he well knew his faults and his unworthiness, nobody better, but suggested that the Divine Mercy might choose to make light of them in view of his unswerving devotion and national record; and promised that if she would only secure this favor for him, she might depend on his doing something for her at the earliest opportunity. He then recited the rosary with the greatest care, never allowing his mind to wander once; and at last, greatly strengthened and comforted, rose to go with a childlike confidence in his prayer being heard.

All through the day this feeling of exaltation persisted, deaf to anything reason could say. He did not remain among the pleasures and excitements of Dublin, but went quietly home, to meditate and wait for news. And late in the afternoon came the hoped-for, the expected, sign that true faith will never be disappointed or betrayed. A woman employee of the tourist office telephoned to say that Mr. Fitzgibbon wished to see him at ten the following day to make the final arrangements.

Unlike so many gratified suitors, Tommy did not immediately forget the source of his benefit, but sat for a long while beside the telephone with clasped hands, pouring out thanks and praise and making all kinds of extravagant vows for the future.

In view of the high and solemn level at which his appointment had been decided, he was somewhat taken aback by Mr. Fitzgibbon's demeanor at their interview. A little smile, which he kept vainly trying to suppress, played continually about his lips; and, on Tommy's first sitting down opposite him, he treated him to a long, thoughtful scrutiny in which considerable amusement mingled with wonder. Yet when at last he spoke, his words left nothing to be desired.

"You're the lad for the job, all right," he said, and the little smile threatened to become a grin. "And now let's talk of sordid things like salaries."

And so here Tommy stood with his friends, shortly to be a salaried man with his own office and a car at his disposal, and graciously received the tributes of his fellow countrymen.

Felix watched the scene for a few moments, smiling happily to himself, and then turned to look at the canvas. As he did so his body stiffened and the smile left his lips, which slowly pursed themselves in a soundless whistle. Next he tried shutting his eyes and warily opening them again to see if that would help, but found that matters remained as before. It was the most bewildering thing he had ever experienced: the Lafuente was undoubtedly hanging there before him, but the general effect of it was somehow completely altered.

"Tommy! Tommy, look," he muttered urgently in the gratified hero's ear. "Do look at the picture."

"I will, of course," Tommy said in his most urbane manner. "That is what we are here for." With a last acknowledgment to his public he turned a connoisseur's eye on the painting. "Isn't it great?" he asked fervently. "I like it better every time I see it."

"Hoo hoo hoo! Hoo hoo hoo!"

Unnoticed by anyone, Mrs. Barry had been quietly swelling and purpling and had now reached the point where she could contain herself no longer. The sound of her enormous mirth easily rode the din of the room, causing heads to turn toward her in consternation. Oblivious of all else, she gave herself up to it with the voluptuous abandon of one who knows that such a joke can never come her way again. Murmurs of resentment began to be heard on all sides.

"Madam, I shall remove you," Felix said severely. With a hand under her elbow he guided her through the crowd, muttering apologies at the angry faces in their path as they went. "Overcome . . . so proud of Mr. O'Driscoll . . . a great moment for us all." The only effect of these was to send the detrimental lady into fresh paroxysms.

"Were you trying to get us lynched?" Felix inquired when they found themselves safely outside. "And pray, what have you been up to?"

"Sh! Here comes Tommy," was her reply as she felt for a pocket handkerchief.

"Are you all right? What was the joke? They didn't like it," Tommy began, looking thoroughly flustered.

" 'They' can go to pot, my dear child," Mrs. Barry retorted briskly, drying her eyes. "What an extraordinary bunch of people. Very sad, when you've known the real Dublin."

"And what was the 'real' Dublin?" Felix asked, laughing in spite of himself.

"When Sahibs ran it," she told him, dismissing the

counterfeit city of today with a wave of her tiny hand.

"The people seem content with it as it is," he teased her.

"I dare say. They seem content with the picture as it is." And at this there was such an alarming return of her symptoms that Felix hurried them all off to luncheon without further ado.

The matter was not alluded to during the meal, which went off in a delightfully carefree way. Tommy was much too pleased with life as a whole to allow the incident to worry him long; and although Felix was, strictly speaking, the host, he explained the menu to Mrs. Barry and suggested what she should eat, with a charming hospitality. He also, for he was in a protective mood, gave her sound advice about the tenant who was to take the Bijou as soon as himself had found accommodation more in keeping with his new responsibilities. Mrs. Barry had run into this character the evening before and was quite entranced with him; he was a Frenchman, true, but a Marquis, who had spent twelve years in the Foreign Legion and had produced three books, at his own expense, he told her, as his writing was too courageous and true to life to appeal to commercial publishers. In fact, the last volume had been seized on a magistrate's order. He wore a Buddhist robe and allowed his hair to fall on his shoulders; and he spoke, for a Frenchman, with an amusingly Cockney accent.

"He may be all right. I'm not saying he isn't," Tommy said to her now with much earnestness. "But you'd best get your rent in advance. There's an awful lot of foreign chancers in Dublin just now."

"Teach your grandmother to suck eggs," she responded merrily. "No one ever made a fool of me yet."

"Ah, but you're so trusting," he sighed; "and some fellows'd take advantage of you."

It was only that evening, when Tommy was safe with his brilliant new friends in the literary bar, that Felix tapped on the door of Mrs. Barry's studio, looking unusually serious and determined. She was stirring some ingredients together in an enormous vat and seemed none too glad of the interruption.

"Alone at last, my proud beauty," he began. "I won't keep you, but you simply have to tell me something. What in thunder did you do to the painting? It's nothing, and yet it's everything. I never could make the picture out at the best of times; but one needn't be an expert to see the imprint of your tiny cloven hoof."

Mrs. Barry looked at him steadily with an infernal gleam in her eye. "I'll answer you that when you've answered me something else."

"Proceed."

"How was it you knew something was up, and Tommy didn't?"

Felix hesitated and took a turn about the room. Then he laughed and shrugged ruefully in token of defeat. "You're a deep one."

"I am, of course." A shocking burst of laughter followed these words.

"Shall we leave it there?"

"Certainly. And now be off with you. I am going to brew some beer."

fourteen

It has often been said in the past that Ireland is a distressful country; and events were about to prove the dictum true again. These events were of a cruel, almost a diabolical, nature. Anyone who turns a passionless eye on Irish history will hardly escape the conclusion that much of its grief could, with some management, have been avoided. The blow that was to dash the cup from Ireland's lips once more did not come into this category; it was a fiendish, fortuitous bolt from the blue.

All Dublin was waiting with blissfully bated breath for what it felt would be the consummation, and indeed the true purpose, of the O'Driscoll raid —namely, the father and mother of a row that should follow. The sudden flowering of artistic awareness, which had led Mr. Paul O'Farrell on more than one occasion confidently to predict an Irish Renaissance, was merely the offshoot of this gleeful anticipation.

Thanks to the heroes of the past, Ireland today was free of the Saxon yoke, as Gaelic as she wished to be and more Catholic than anyone would have thought possible; but she was also hideously dull. Not only would the episode provide a refreshing break in the monotony, but if, as was to be feared, the chicanery backed up by unprincipled might of the foe were to prevail, she could look forward to a long spell of the aggrieved recrimination in which she felt so particularly at home.

It was no wonder, then, that sparkling eyes and happy faces were seen all over the town.

So far there had not been so much as a whisper from the London side. Those in the know, which included practically everyone, were able to reveal the reason for this—namely, that the matter had gone to the highest Cabinet levels. The truth was that Sir Alvary had his hands full for the moment with a forthcoming exhibition of Chinese prints. It was was the sort of luck that had followed him blindly throughout his career, and which he always referred to, in a hushed voice, as Providence.

One morning there appeared in *The Times* a letter which ran as follows:

Sir:

Much has been written of recent times about the "Goat" pictures of the Spanish painter, Afrodisio Lafuente y Chaos. Of the artistic qualities of these I do not speak, but I feel that English readers should know of the appalling circumstances under which these pictures were obtained. A very old friend of mine, now unhappily dead, knew the painter well, and indeed had a villa adjoining his in Campo del Flor.

For weeks together the painter would remain inert,

merely drinking and strumming idly on a guitar. But when the fit was on him he would paint for four or five days on end, neither eating nor sleeping. For all that period the unhappy goats who served as his models were lashed to a contraption of his own devising which, my friend assured me, she could only liken to an instrument of medieval torture. Their piteous cries for mercy would make her blood run cold. At least one wretched animal expired from pain and heat. Another that proved recalcitrant had a horn knocked off, the painter having thrown at it a bronze effigy of St. Francis of Assissi. My friend's attempts to rouse the Spanish authorities to a proper sense of their duty was met with that smiling indifference to the animal world which alas! characterizes this otherwise excellent people. The mental affliction that clouded her latter days is believed to have been due, at least in part, to her experience at this time.

Those who hurry to admire the undoubted genius of this wicked man would do well to ponder these facts. "Is it nothing to all ye who pass by?"

I am, Sir, &c.

Rosemary Horniman

Villa Sevenoaks
San Miguel
Torremolinos

The readers of *The Times* are an unpredictable race. That they are fundamentally serious, informed and responsible cannot be in doubt, since otherwise they would not be reading *The Times*. Yet while it is a perfectly simple matter to forecast, almost word for word, what the leader-writers are going to say in any situation whatever, the correspondence column follows a dance of its own.

The response to the Horniman letter conformed

to this old tradition. Whether because of the quiet, typically British understatement of the letter itself; or because the Editor's mailbag held nothing else of interest that day—unless a leading scientist's warning of the probable obliteration of the British Isles by hydrogen bombs could be so described; or for some other, obscurely psychological, reason, there was a volume of protest unequaled since that which raged at the time of Adolf Hitler's entry into Prague, when the subject had been the shooting of rooks.

This of itself would have had little effect on Sir Alvary Wilberforce. He paid scant attention to the views of the public, whom he catalogued, readers of *The Times* and all, as "the heathen." He liked what he called good painting, and Afrodisio Lafuente was what he called a good painter; there, for him, the matter began and ended. If cranks wished to boycott the Gallery on the word, impossible at this stage to verify, of some crazed old woman, Sir Alvary was quite prepared in his bluff English way to tell them where they could go.

He would have been prepared to do so, rather, had it not been for Lady Wilberforce. Sir Alvary in his public capacity was a different being from Sir Alvary in the bosom of his family. One of the things that characterized him abroad, for example, was a fine flow of nervous English; but those privileged to see him at home were astounded to find that his utterances there restricted themselves largely to "Yes, m'dear," "No, m'dear" and "I feel sure you are right, m'dear." Lady Wilberforce held not only the opinions of a right-thinking Englishwoman about animals and foreigners, but also a life membership in the British Goat Society. She possessed seventy goats or more at their country house and made no secret of preferring them to the majority of her acquaintance. Her discussion with Sir Alvary now was brief, incisive and even by Wilberforce standards unilateral; the upshot of it was that the two Lafuente paintings were bundled into the Gallery cellar from alleged lack of space. No formal statement was made about the third, but the story somehow got about, and was never denied, that its return would not be pressed for.

"Hate to let the beggars get away with it, m'dear," Sir Alvary vouchsafed one evening at dinner, in the dispirited mumble that, under his own roof, replaced his habitual roar.

"They are of no importance whatever, Alvary," was her ladyship's firm reply as she helped him to pudding. "It is a question of right and wrong. Other considerations are irrelevant."

The effect of this turn of affairs on Dublin opinion is not easy to describe and would be impossible to exaggerate. Not since the Germans dropped a land mine there during the dark days of the "Emergency" had anti-British feeling run as high. A rumor at once went into circulation that Miss Horniman's letter was one of those clever forgeries that the English invariably produce when trying to save their faces; but, curious to say, it never really took hold. Over the capital there settled a dull despair, the despair of a small, defenseless people to whom Fate has given a neighbor ruthless, powerful and dead to the claims of ordinary decency.

The keen interest in art which had so delighted Mr. O'Farrell withered away at once. In the shortest time the attendance at the House of Irish Painting shrank to normal; and one morning the manager telephoned to Mr. Roche, fretfully desiring him to "Take the thing away."

"We need the space," he said.

"Ah, now," Tacky pleaded. He was working hard on plans for the Prado cafeteria and had little time to spare for theoretical issues. "Sure, what harm is it doing? And, anyway, wasn't the room kept empty for it?"

"That's what I mean," the other said. "It's kept empty as a dignified protest against its non-return; and with the way things are, we think, and a certain crowd agree with us, that it is psychologically confusing for the people to see it there."

"Hang on to it for a whileen more," Tacky urged him. "Anyway, till I get a word with the Cŏmmĭttēē."

"And when do you suppose you'll get that?"

"It's a bad time of year just now, with the members going on holidays," Tacky parried. "But I won't forget you!"

He hung up the receiver with the firm intention of doing nothing at all.

At the time of the letter's publication, Miss Philomena Scully had just embarked on her annual Retreat. In spite of the abstinence it imposed upon her, she enjoyed the occasion more than anything else in life and for three happy weeks reveled in contemplation of the fallen state of the world and in confessions, of inordinate length and astonishing detail, of her own part in the same. From it she would emerge, sustained and refreshed and without her customary hang-over, to resume her battle with Satan.

As soon as she read Miss Horniman's disclosure

she saw how urgently needed her military experience was, and she gave poor Tacky no peace until he had called yet another Meeting Extraordinary of the Committee for the Irish Temple of Art.

When the members had forgathered, Tacky announced in his weariest tone that they had done so at the request of one member, Miss Scully, and he invited her without more ado to reveal what she had in mind.

"I propose a resolution," that lady said, opening her traplike mouth peculiarly wide, "that this Committee rejects the painting of Lafuente on behalf of the Temple of Art and dissociates itself emphatically from all that has taken place in connection with it."

"Hear hear!" said Lady Twomey. Unnatural as it was for her to agree with Miss Scully, in the light of Munnings and Birmingham she could do no less.

Miss Scully felt keenly disappointed. Her general war with evil was carried on by skirmishes with the individuals she saw as embodying it, and she had taken it for granted that on this occasion, as always, Lady Twomey would stand in for the Devil. She now remarked, with a toss of her head, that she was very gratified.

"We may not see eye to eye in matters of art," Lady Twomey proceeded, developing her position, "but when it comes to the ill treatment of helpless dumb creatures, there can be no two opinions."

"Oh, *that!*" exclaimed Miss Scully, in happy relief.

"What do you mean, *that?* What else can you be referring to?"

"I object, as I hope any decent Catholic would, to the exhibition in a Catholic country of work by a man in the habit of using holy images as missiles." Miss Scully had rehearsed this lapidary indictment on the way to the meeting, and she rattled it off at impressive speed.

"Really!" Lady Twomey leaned back in her chair with a tired but indulgent smile.

"Yes, really, Lady Twomey. It will probably surprise you, but there really are some people who object to blasphemy and sacrilege. Believe it or not, there really is some decency left."

"I am not sure if I care for your tone, Miss Scully."

"Ladies!" The Chairman appeared to be feeling unwell. "Do I understand then, Lady Twomey, that you withdraw your support of the resolution?"

"No; but I entirely dissociate myself from the mover's reason for it."

"That'll sound well, if it gets about," Mr. Mac-Mahon observed, nervously smoothing his hair.

"And I entirely dissociate myself from any Committee with blasphemers and pagans on it!" Miss Scully's voice was dangerously shrill.

"Would that mean," asked Tacky, catching at a little straw of hope, "that you resign?"

"It would!" Nothing had been further from Miss Scully's intention, but she was borne along on the tide of her own dialectic.

Hitherto Mr. Connolly had been a mere passenger on the forward march of the Committee. He was no more clear as to why he had joined it than as to why he should have been asked to do so, and the proceedings themselves had mystified him altogether. He had been content to sit patiently and to listen, and to vote in any way that seemed expected; but now he had a sudden, happy inspiration.

"Why don't we all resign?" he asked.

For nearly a minute the Committee was too astonished to speak. The possibility had never so much as occurred to a single member. Of them all only Tacky had any definite plans concerning the Irish Prado itself; the two ladies had regarded the whole affair as a means of self-expression, while the men had vaguely felt that committees were good things to be on, and feared that if they declined the honor somebody else would get it. Once it was formed, they had gone steadily on without any misgiving at all; and yet Mr. Connolly's proposal, when the first shock of it was over, attracted them strangely.

"And all our work to go for nothing?" Seumas Cullen hesitated.

"What work?"

There was no reply.

Tacky's fertile brain was working at full stretch. For some time past there had been slowly taking shape in his mind the idea that once all his subsidiary schemes for the Prado were realized, the problem of how to fill it would not be so very grave after all. What Ireland urgently needed, for example, was a first-class skating rink; if he could use the largest hall for this, instead of scratching around for paintings and statues, it would kill two birds with one stone. To dissolve the present Committee and form another one, better attuned to the needs and aspirations of the Irish people, with himself still in charge, would be a fine step on the way to it; further, it would let him out of the shindy about the Spanish fellow; and accordingly he arranged his features in an expression of dignified self-sacrifice.

"If it should be your wish, I'll not stand in the way," he said quietly. "I'll not push myself forward."

"I think all here will agree we couldn't have had a

better Chairman," Mr. MacMahon said with warmth; and there was a little burst of applause.

"Then will you each write me a letter?" Tacky requested, on the same subdued note. "And I'll attend to the rest. It only remains to thank the lot of you for your public-spirited service. I'm sure the country ought to be grateful."

With these expressions of mutual esteem and good will the Committee took leave of each other for the last time. Mr. Connolly, suddenly a man of consequence, went by invitation with Mr. MacMahon and Seumas Cullen for a jar. Lady Twomey proceeded to her Club, in the hope of a game of bridge. Exhausted by the efforts of the afternoon and aware of the emotional gap that now stood in her life, Miss Scully went straight to bed with a bottle. Tacky remained in his office blithely drafting the new proposal.

But the fates had another shot in their locker yet. Simultaneously with the dissolution of the Committee, there came a new and disquieting development in regard to the Prado itself. The strike among the workmen continued, nor did there seem any chance of an early settlement; and now an architect who had unsuccessfully put in for the contract observed with delight, while driving past the skeleton building, that there was a definite tilt to it. One end was sinking into the ground already, and what would happen when the whole affair was completed was anyone's guess. The architect, as a responsible citizen, lost no time in bringing the matter to the attention of the authorities, and another appalling row ensued. Summoned to give an account of himself, the architect in charge almost tearfully defended the validity of his blueprint and the soundness of his execution; what had happened, he thought, was that some complicated and unforeseeable change in geological structure had tilted the ground itself, making the building appear out of alignment, although this could not be the case. His explanation was badly received, however, and it was decided to hold an inquiry.

Rumors were already buzzing about the city, and an official statement to the effect that they were unfounded removed the last doubt from the people's minds. In the normal way their reaction to the situation would have been clear and uniform. There would have been private joy and mirth, public indignation and short shrift for any foreigner who ventured to pass a remark. As things were, it followed too close on the heels of Miss Horniman's letter and filled the national cup of woe and humiliation to the brim. There did indeed appear to be an evil spell on Ireland; and even substantial middle-class men began to speak of emigration. Mr. O'Farrell himself, who had redoubled his efforts since the committal of Seán O'Hara, now sat listlessly at home reading murder stories all day long. Such little confidence in the nation's leaders as had ever existed now dwindled to nothing; and the general feeling was best summed up by the comment of Mr. Mervyn Roche, when he learned of the death of his hopes.

"Wouldn't they make you tired?" he asked simply, and, cutting his losses with the courage and resolution he invariably displayed, he got to work at once on a scheme for a mammoth greyhound track.

fifteen

Old Peadar sat on a fallen tree by the edge of the brook and composed a letter. He had chosen this place to write in because of the private nature of his communication. It was the second letter he had written in fifteen years; like the first, it was to be anonymous and, also like the first, it was called forth by the treatment of himself by Mrs. Barry.

The previous missive had enjoyed a great success and caused a wide repercussion. This had been directed at Mrs. Barry in person and reviled her in a manly, straight-forward way for her treatment of those unfortunate enough to work for her. In that year there had been an exceptionally hot spell and, missing her Indian comforts, she had set Peadar to work as punkah wallah. At the time of writing he had been the only Christian actually in her employ; and as he read his indictment over, it struck him that the mere omission of his own name might not, in the circumstances, sufficiently mask his identity. He decided therefore to omit hers as well, and posted the letter addressed simply to "The Biggest Old Bitch in Ballyknock," never dreaming that there could be any doubt as to who this was. But when Mrs. Mathew, the Postmistress, was sorting the letters, she assumed at once that the appellation could only be intended for her mortal foe, the village dressmaker; accordingly, and without fully considering her position, she penciled the words "Try Miss Deirdre O'Sullivan" across the envelope and gave it to the postman.

Miss O'Sullivan consulted a solicitor, who assured her that she had a promising case. Between them they concocted a horrifying letter to Mrs. Mathew, which threatened her with proceedings in Court and estimated the damage to Miss O'Sullivan's hitherto unblemished repute at a minimum of fifteen hundred pounds. Mrs. Mathew was quite unmoved by the latter notion, as all she possessed in the world was two hundred and seventeen pounds and, furthermore, no one knew that she had those; but she was anxious to avoid scandal and so she consulted a solicitor in her turn. After much correspondence and with a fine show of reluctance, Miss O'Sullivan agreed to accept a five-pound note and a written apology in full settlement of her claim; and, even if the ladies loved each other none the better, there matters could have been expected to lie.

Passing Miss O'Sullivan's cottage a day or so later, Mrs. Mathew was appalled to find her letter prominently displayed in the window. It had been glued to a sheet of white cardboard, and above it was written in large red capitals: "How Are the Mighty Fallen!" In view of the undoubted injury to the complaining party, Mrs. Mathew had taken her solicitor's advice and expressed her regret in a humble, fulsome manner that contrasted notably with her style of every day; and to find this misleading text exposed to the mirth of the village was too much for her spirit to bear. Having bought, and studied, a popular handbook on law, she came to the conclusion that this was a Breach of Copyright and she instructed her solicitor, despite anything he could say, to write to Miss O'Sullivan in this sense. Further correspondence raged between the parties and ended only when the document in question fell down of its own accord. Miss O'Sullivan never replaced it, letting it be known that she had better things to think about.

Since this day, now many years past, the pair had never exchanged a word. At considerable inconvenience to herself, Miss O'Sullivan posted all her letters in the next village seven miles away, and Mrs. Mathew continued diligently to peruse her legal handbook in the faith that sometime, by its means, she would catch her enemy out.

Peadar had been so gratified by the results of his action that he had never set pen to paper since, thinking that to do so could only lead to an anticlimax. Yet Mrs. Barry's latest offense had been so heinous as to leave him no alternative, if he wished to call himself a man, but to seek revenge. She had accused him, in so many words and to his face, of "pinching" her eggs! Him, a poor man dependent on his fair name for a livelihood! Apart from its bitterly wounding him, the charge was quite unfounded, for the daily collection of eggs from the nesting-boxes was of all his duties the one to which he devoted the greatest care.

These boxes were of such extraordinary shapes and sizes and in such varying states of repair, and were dotted about in such curious situations, that with the best will of fowl and man a certain number of eggs were always found to be cracked when the time came to gather them up. Of this Mrs. Barry was well aware, and to this she was perfectly resigned, and there had always been a tacit agreement that the damaged specimens should go to Peadar. Some time ago however, possibly because the hens were gaining experience with the boxes, there had begun a steady falling-off in their number, until Peadar at last had seen there was nothing for it, in equity, but to attend to the cracking himself.

For a while he had scrupulously maintained the normal ratio, which had been roughly three in a dozen, but as the days went by he began to feel that this arrangement was arbitrary and unnatural. He now commenced to crack more on some evenings than on others, as being more in harmony with the mysterious fluctuations of Fate itself, only to discover that this method also failed in that when the turn come round for cracking less he felt an unaccountable spiritual revulsion from doing so. Almost without his noticing it, the numbers crept up until the positions were reversed and Mrs. Barry was receiving three eggs of each dozen instead of nine; and it was then that, suddenly and with a brutal disregard of the pain and embarrassment it must cause him, she had taxed him with "pinching" them.

"Are you suggesting, ma'am," he cried, looking her full in the eye with the quiet assurance that only an easy conscience can give, "that I ever took what wasn't my own?"

"I'm saying you're the finest old blackguard in the

country!" And she marched away, deaf to Peadar's remonstrances and his entreaties to the holy angels in heaven that they appear forthwith and give evidence on his behalf.

Twenty minutes later, as her custom was, she had forgiven and forgotten the whole affair; but Peadar had not, and he cast about in his mind for a way of doing her harm. His first natural impulse was to fire the toolshed, but he controlled it, since, with the queer old mood Mrs. Barry was in, she might easily suspect him. A dream of poisoning one of her dogs had similarly to be renounced; indeed, the problem of safeguarding himself teased him as much as that of injuring her.

Presently an idea struck him of such brilliance as fairly took away his breath. Peadar knew, as the whole village knew, the story of the picture and how it had lodged for a while in Mrs. Barry's house; and he also knew, as no one else did, that she had been up to some divilment with it. He had been cleaning windows in the attic one day, and wasn't she at it with the paints and the brushes and laughing away to herself as if her wits were gone? He was too used to her capers to think much of it at the time, nor had he then realized the picture's importance, as the affair had not been made public; but it now came vividly back to his memory and he felt sure he could get her into trouble. A vision of his tormentor marching away between two Guards flitted through his mind and entranced him. With an intelligent industry he could never have brought to any of his usual employments, he read the newspapers back to discover the whereabouts of the canvas and the name of its official custodian, and now, safe in this lonely spot, he wrote slowly and painfully as follows:

Mister, I pen these lines as a sincear Irishman and not because of what she done to me. You ought to look at that picture that was in all the papers. I seen her adulteratin it with the paints the whole of an evenin. That won does not fere God or man, and she laughin fit to bust. Please to keep me out of it, being a poor man and tormented to blazes with her. May she burn in hell, pleas God.

Yours sincearly,
A sincear Irishman

The letter satisfied him when he had finished it as being both informative and discreet, and he lost no time in bringing it to the post. Afterwards he worried a little as to whether she would continue to pay his wages while she languished in jail; but on the whole he was well content and awaited the outcome with serene anticipation.

His cup would have been full indeed could he have known what was to follow, although once again things turned out quite differently from his intention. The letter was delivered and read and was on the point of being consigned to the wastepaper basket with various others when, for no clear reason, the recipient checked himself and read it again. A curious uneasiness filled his mind as he did so. He had been present throughout the triumphal opening of this special exhibit, and the tiny figure of Mrs. Barry, shaking with uncontrollable and unexplained laughter, lingered unpleasantly in his memory. He had no idea who she was, but she had apparently come with young Thomas O'Driscoll; what in Heaven's name, then, could she have been laughing at? Was there something fishy about the business? And why were the English not proceeding in it?

These anxious thoughts flitted through his head one after the other as he read. "Adulteratin it with the paints . . ."; but it was impossible. They had the word of Mr. O'Farrell, with all the weight of his European reputation behind it, that the picture was a perfect specimen of the master's art. Despite that reputation, however, he now crammed Peadar's missive into his pocket and hastened almost at a run to the room, deserted these days, where the picture stood. For a long while he peered at the canvas, with eyes open and eyes half shut, from close to and from a distance, until at last he drew a long, deep breath of relief. He did not pretend, at any rate to himself, to any familiarity with Lafuente's work, but even he could see that nothing had been recently added. Whoever had painted this picture, it had been done all at the same time and by the same hand; of that there could be no doubt at all.

With all the clear evidence of his eyes before him, he nevertheless remained apprehensive. "And she laughin fit to bust . . ."; those were ominous words, all right. He had his full share of the Irish dread of laughter, and the thought of anyone, anywhere, for whatever reason, enjoying a joke even partly at his expense afflicted him with almost a physical pain. Convinced as he was that there was no need for it, he nevertheless craved reassurance; he must share this burden with someone, take the second opinion of a qualified party without Mr. O'Farrell's getting to hear of it, and obtain from him the *nihil obstat* which should set his mind at rest. And then he bethought himself of the German fellow.

The visit of Dr. Horst von Gudenus to Dublin had proved something of a disappointment. When through the Irish grapevine in London it had been reported that he was coming, it was accepted as the most natural thing in the world. This distinguished Kunsthistoriker was known to have carried out a tour of the major collections of Europe that spring, and that his tour should culminate in Ireland was seen as eminently fitting. Those concerned held themselves ready to welcome him in the traditional way with feasting and merriment, to display to him the artistic treasures of the capital, to slip into his ears a few judicious words of Irish propaganda and to clear up for him any little queries of a scholastic nature that he might care to raise; and on hearing of his arrival at the Shelbourne Hotel they had sat back, in some complacency, and waited for him to present his introductions.

To their surprise, he did nothing of the kind. The days went by and he appeared in none of the places where he was expected. The hotel was discreetly approached, but could give no account of him beyond the fact that he was usually out. At last they could bear it no longer and, after consultation, suggested to one of the reporters that an interview might assist in clarifying the situation. The German received the man with jovial courtesy and praised many features of Dublin life, notably the beer, but when he was asked for his opinion of the national collections the reply came as a fresh surprise.

"To tell you the truth, I have not seen them," he smilingly answered. "I am—how do you say it?— taking things easy."

"On holidays, then?" the reporter asked, his face falling.

"Not exactly that," Dr. von Gudenus told him. "I am here for the purpose of seeing once again my old nurse. Ah, that good, kind, simple woman! She is a real credit to you. Ireland is known on the Continent for two things above all: in the first line, the Sweepstake, and in the second, the good, kind nurses. We spend our days in her kitchen together, talking over the old times and drinking cups of tea."

This statement did not appear in the paper.

To the troubled man at the House of Irish Painting the much-criticized aloofness of the German scholar was an extra reason for getting hold of him. At all costs he must avoid starting any talk or his life would simply be not worth living. He telephoned to the Shelbourne Hotel next morning early, before Dr. von Gudenus had time to set out for his nurse, and with many apologies for the intrusion, asked if there was any likelihood of his having a few moments to spare that day. The authenticity of one of the paintings in his care had been called in question; he was himself in two minds about it, but it was not his period and so, unwilling as he was to inconvenience anyone, he should be more grateful than words could say for another opinion.

"I come at once, of course," the German said cheerfully. "And the picture? What is the picture?"

"One of the 'Goat' pictures of Afrodisio Lafuente, a modern Spanish; perhaps you've heard of him?"

A mighty German laugh came booming along the wire. "Ach so, I did hear something indeed. My poor old friend Sir Wilberforce!" Dr. von Gudenus shouted gleefully. "We have laughed so much with this. Yes, but look! I have seen these paintings in London, and there is no doubt of them."

"Well, authenticity was a manner of speaking. Frankly, there is a suggestion in certain quarters that the painting was tampered with in some way. Wouldn't it be just like the English to play a trick like that?"

"They did not know you were coming, my friend," said the German, laughing again. "But don't worry. I come now. I am all—how do you say it?—agog."

The man at the Gallery afterwards looked back to the German's visit as one of the most appalling experiences of his life. Dr. von Gudenus filled him with confidence from the moment he appeared: his keen blue eyes, his careful English, the well-polished shoes and the black portfolio under his arm all seemed to indicate a sound artistic formation; and the pleasantly calm tone in which, when the greetings were over, he inquired, "And now where is the patient?" had a wonderfully soothing effect on his nerves. He led him without further ado to the Lafuente, already visualizing the moment when, after scanning the picture with German thoroughness, the scholar would turn around and assure him that his fears were groundless. So sure of the verdict was he that phrases of regret for the gentleman's wasted time were ready on the end of his tongue. But the nicely chosen words were never spoken. With a provoking deliberation, Dr. von Gudenus drew out a pair of spectacles, cleaned them, set them on his nose and looked steadily at the canvas; for about five seconds his face wore an expression of utter amazement and then, with a stentorian cry of, *"Ach Du lieber Gott, ist doch unmöglich!"* he exploded in a series of guffaws of a sustained power with which Mrs. Barry herself could never have hoped to compete.

"My poor friend," he said at last to the horror-stricken man beside him, choking helplessly over the words, "I am so happy to tell you that this picture is quite all right. No one has added so much as the stroke of a brush. So much really you could have seen for yourself. But don't you agree on the whole"—and, lifting the picture up, he turned it swiftly around and held it out in the new position—"that it looks better like this?"

"It was . . . upside down?" stammered its guardian with dry lips.

"I am afraid so."

The silence that followed was so profound that a bubble might have been heard collapsing. Then there was a wild clutch at a straw of possible justification.

"But the signature! Look at the signature! We went by the signature!"

"Yes, yes," sighed the German, examining it. "Strictly, I should not have said that no one had added a stroke. Look here. There the signature was once; and here it is now. Someone has been very clever! Very clever indeed, and even more naughty. A little joke. You are fond of little jokes in Ireland, no?"

"Only when they are funny," his companion informed him in a voice like the east wind.

"We Germans have not your keen sense of humor," Dr. von Gudenus said thoughtfully, "but it seems to me quite a nice little joke. I was reading some of your critics on this painting. Yes, not a bad little joke. But I am wrong, perhaps. I shall ask my old friend, Sir Wilberforce."

At these words the Irishman blenched. The broad Teutonic face before him swam in a pink mist and the entire room appeared to rise and fall and revolve like a merry-go-round. "Ah no, ah no!" he pleaded faintly. "Don't tell that one. Sure, he'd die laughing!"

"I am sure," the German agreed. "And why not? Sir Wilberforce is perhaps a little stupid, but he is what you call a good old stick. And he loves painting. How many of the people who came to see the Lafuente loved painting? And how many of them just wanted to laugh? I must admit that when I heard of this matter I, too, laughed—how do you say it?—like a drain. And now it seems that the joke is even better than we supposed. Why is Sir Wilberforce not to enjoy it with us?"

"Look, Doctor," the other urged him desperately, "we're a young country. Mind you, I wouldn't say this to everyone, but there's a certain amount we have to learn. We were kept down. The English never gave us a chance. And if they ever get to hear of this," he wound up, his eyes distended with horror, "they'll be absolutely delighted! Do you know what that Wilberforce fellow said of us? He had yet to meet an Irishman that knew a Lafuente from a cow's tail!" And he gazed intently at the German to observe the effect of this enormity on him.

"There perhaps he went a little far," said Dr. von Gudenus judicially. "The differences between the two are such as to make the possibility of confusion extremely remote. But, if I may say so, there seems to be some foundation for his little quip."

"Sure, wasn't the bloody thing passed for us by Mr. Paul O'Farrell?"

"Who is Mr. Paul O'Farrell, please? I have not heard this name."

"Not heard of Mr. Paul O'Farrell? The connoisseur? Why, he's famous! He'd have been Director of

the Temple of Art, only that there isn't going to be one. Paul O'Farrell is known all over Europe."

"Except, apparently, in Düsseldorf." The German smiled. "And so I am to behave like a gentleman. *Ach weh!* The 'gentleman' is the worst thing the English ever thought of, worse than their custard. Behaving like one is invariably inconvenient or disagreeable or expensive; and very often all three. So, I leave you. Poor Nanny will wonder where I am. Goodbye!" He removed his spectacles and turned to go. "Oh, and by ze way," he said casually, over his shoulder, "when people have a certain amount to learn, they should lose no time in making a start."

At any other time the impertinence of such a remark would have been justly resented, but our man was too flurried at present even to notice it. On finding himself alone once more, his first thought was to make an act of humble thanksgiving to Him who had stayed his hand as it was about to throw Peadar's letter away. He registered a vow on the spot never to scorn communications of the kind in future. He next considered the position as a whole and found nothing in it of comfort. He was nicely stuck with the body, all right; Tacky had vanished out of his life like a mist in the morning sun, in the way he always did when the going was rough. The mere thought of breaking the news to Mr. O'Farrell made him feel quite weak. On his shoulders alone rested the decision of what to do now; and only the good faith of the German—was he to be trusted?—could save Ireland from becoming the laughing-stock of the world.

"Isn't it us all over?" he muttered to the room at large with intense bitterness. "Oasis of Christian culture, how are you?"

Well, there was no time to be lost in repining. The

great thing was to prevent the story from leaking out. He would breathe not a word of it to a soul, not even to his subordinates in the Gallery, but bury it away in his bosom forever. The only secrets kept in Ireland were the ones that nobody knew. With sudden energy he turned the picture face to the wall. Next he pulled the blinds over the windows and went away, locking the door behind him and removing the key from the ring. It would have been a relief to throw it in the river. He wrote a notice, "Closed for Necessary Repairs," in his own hand and came back himself to fix it on the door, glancing about him as nervously as a burglar while he did so. The picture would at least be safe from prying eyes until he had worked out a plan.

These immediate steps accomplished, he felt curiously parched and debilitated, and although eleven had barely struck he thought he had better step out for a quiet glass of something. He walked with the deliberate air and the hesitant gait of a man who in fact is running away. It was a habit with him to use a particular bar in a side street quite some distance off, as he wished his staff to believe that he did not drink at all; and as a rule this bar was much frequented by steady professional men with the same aspiration. Even for them, however, it was still rather early, and as he came in the barman, languidly massaging the marble counter with a dirty rag, looked up in surprise.

"Morning, Mr. Moran. The usual?"

"If you please. No, wait there!" he cried on a sudden impulse. "What's usual about this? I'll have a ball of malt."

"You're my first customer," said the man, hoping

to draw him out as he poured the whiskey. "Water, Mr. Moran?"

"No, thanks." Mr. Moran drained the glass at one gulp and held it out again, "Fill me up, will you? I think it tasted all right, but I want to make sure."

The barman laughed politely. Mr. Moran took somewhat longer with his second drink and gazed pensively into its tawny depths as if expecting to find the riddle of life explained there.

"Do you know something, Micky," he began lugubriously, after a while. "My father was a policeman."

"Is that right, Mr. Moran? So was mine."

"Have a drink on it," Mr. Moran commanded, emptying his glass once more, "and give me one. A simple policeman. Never promoted. Nothing wrong in that, is there?"

"Not at all, Mr. Moran," came in Micky's dulcet voice. "I like my own trade better, all the same."

"Do you so?" said Mr. Moran with a hyena-like laugh. "I don't, then!"

"Yerra, go on, Mr. Moran! And you with a big position, that you made for yourself with your own talents!"

"My own talents, says he!" The liquor sent the blood coursing through Mr. Moran's veins, filling him with warmth and irresponsible ease and slyly detaching one by one the bonds that held him captive to bleak reality. "Micky boy, there isn't talent in the whole of Ireland to cover a sixpence."

"Ah, that's right now; slap the poor old place!"

"It's true, though. Fill up, there's the lad." He sat communing with himself awhile. "I'll tell you something now," he said presently, "that I wouldn't tell another. And I wouldn't tell you, only for your being a policeman's son. And mind, it's under the most sacred seal of the confessional. You'll ruin the lot of us if it ever gets about."

"I'll not mention it, Mr. Moran, of course."

"You know the picture down at my place, the one that we got from the English. Do you know what we did with it, after that O'Driscoll lad went through fire and water to bring it? We hung it upside down."

"Sure, what does that matter?" Micky soothed him. "Wouldn't these old pictures today look as well in any position?"

"Christ, Micky, is that the best you can say? There wasn't a soul among us spotted anything wrong. Half Dublin was in there. And we'd never have been any wiser, to the end of time, only a German art fellow looked in and told us."

"Ah, it takes the Continent," Micky agreed, wagging his head with a melancholy sigh.

"And, if you don't mind, Mr. bloody Paul O'Farrell giving out to the papers!" The scorn in Mr. Moran's voice was lethal. "The glorious Mediterranean lucidity! A perfect specimen of the master's something or other period! Treatment of the light in relation to the animal's hide! Guff, the lot of it! There's a fellow that's sunk forever, if the story goes round."

"Ah, God help him, the decent man!" But the barman spoke abstractedly, for more customers now were trickling into the place and he was bursting to spread this delicious item of news without delay. From the corner of his eye he saw Mr. O'Dwyer, O'Farrell's crony, taking up his usual position at the very end of the bar, and decided at once to give him priority. "Ought you to take any more, Mr. Moran, at this time of the morning?" he asked, with the brotherly solicitude for his regulars that made him such a favorite.

"You're right of course, Micky, right as a trivet. I'm gone! Back to the vale of tears. And, Micky, by all that's holy, not a word to a breathing soul. Not even to make conversation. We're all dead men if you open your gob!"

"Mr. Moran, now would I?" plaintively asked the barman. "May the curse of the crows be on me if I spill as much as a word!"

And Mr. Moran returned to his duty, much fortified now and with peace in his heart.

sixteen

On the very day of these happenings, there was to take place an event which also was out of the ordinary run. Tommy O'Driscoll had invited Felix to luncheon and he had gone so far as to suggest they meet at Jammet's. It was the first time in his life that he had asked anyone to a meal, let alone Felix, whom he had always looked on as a natural provider; but solemn occasions call for appropriate measures, and at last Felix was going away.

For some little while now Mr. Horniman had been feeling restless. No one enjoyed Ireland better than he, and no one had extracted more amusement out of the curious affair of the Lafuente in all its aspects. But that was all over, as he believed, and he had also run through the simple diversions and pleasures that Dublin could offer. Now he pined for the sophistication of London and to see the faces of his countless friends light up, as they always did when he appeared, and to hear them exclaim, "Where on earth have you been?" Through this escapade of his he had even missed Ascot, the only time he had ever done such a thing since reaching the years of discretion, and Goodwood would be upon him before he could turn round. He began to reproach himself for idleness and frivolity.

These vaguely accumulating discontents came to a head one night after a vivid and entertaining dream. He was driving round and round St. Stephen's Green in the Daimler, with the little gray monkey from India seated beside him; the creature kept up a ceaseless flow of patter in the florid and inaccurate style of a Babu, until he suddenly broke off, laid a tiny paw on Felix's arm and with a piteous note in his voice inquired, "Am I really all that plain?" Felix burst out laughing in his sleep and woke himself up, still chuckling drowsily as he lay in bed. Now that he finally knew of whom it was that Tommy reminded him, he marveled that anything so obvious should have puzzled him for so long. And one idea led to another and he saw that, charming as this little encounter had been, he had sucked it dry; and, with no more compunction than a swallow might feel in autumn, decided it was time the chapter ended.

On the following day he announced his plans for an early departure, and Tommy was much offended. By a strange coincidence, he, too, had dreamed of Felix in the previous night, and even, too, that they were driving in the Daimler together; and Felix had told him that he was the grandest fellow he had ever met in his life, and had offered him an introduction to Miss Prunella Gibbing. "A million is not to be sneezed at, all the same," he had said, "and you deserve to get it, if anyone does." In the fullness of his grateful heart, Tommy had taken his hand off the steering wheel and pressed it to his lips. How life-like and natural it all had been! And how clearly the scene had stayed in his mind after he woke, filling him with a vague but delightful anticipation! Yet after all that and as cool as you please, Mr. Horniman now simply remarked that it was high time he "pushed off." You never knew where you were with the fellow.

"Don't let me stand in your way," he said icily.

"Oh, you'll never miss me now," Felix replied, glancing with amusement at the little figure, dressed today in a neat gray flannel suit that they had care-fully chosen together. Tommy petulantly tossed his flaming curls and said no more.

For a day or so after that he saw nothing of his rest-less friend. Although he had not yet taken up his new appointment he had already moved to a flat in Balls-bridge, believing that a good town address was es-sential to a man of his future standing. The Royal Dublin Society was only a few minutes' walk away, and the whole neighborhood had an air of genteel solvency that amazed and enchanted him. He was the contented lord of two prettily furnished rooms, a kitchen and a bathroom both provided with geysers that worked, and the key to a garden whose color scheme of red, white and blue did not provoke him as much as might have been feared. Felix had guaran-teed the rent of this place, for a morbid delicacy for-bade Tommy to approach Mrs. Barry and he felt it was early days to raise such points with his new em-ployer; and here, after their little tiff, he remained and brooded, leaving it to the other man to make overtures if he so desired.

Presently Felix did come, but it was a Felix so distraught and so wretched that Tommy's pique all vanished at once. The tale that was stammered out to him did not, in truth, appear as very dreadful, but his warm little heart responded as ever to the sight of human woe; and he told himself, using one of the expressions he had picked up recently, that it would be a sad old world if we all thought the same. The redoubtable Miss Horniman, after a period of unwonted quiescence where her nephew was concerned, had written repeating her invitation of the spring, except that now it was for six whole weeks and was couched in terms that made a refusal impossible. She should expect him, she firmly wrote, by the middle of the following week.

"Six weeks!" Felix said hollowly. "At the very busiest time of the year!" The despair in that usually blithe voice was horrible to the ears of anyone who wished its owner well. "Goodwood, eh?" he ejaculated with a little moan. "Why, I shall have to look sharp if I'm not to miss the Twelfth! I know Aunt Rosemary and her idea of six weeks. How people can live without a single thought for anything but their own wishes and their own pleasures is quite beyond me. I find it extremely odd. She has been like that all her life; and my father was the same. I shall have to leave almost at once!" he cried, finishing his sentence on a falsetto note, such was the power of feeling behind it. "Her letter was sent on from London to the Club, and I haven't been in there for a couple of days. No time to plan or arrange or put people off! That's my Aunt Rosemary all over."

It was then that, carried away by the emotion of the moment, Tommy blurted out his invitation to a farewell banquet, the best that money could buy and entirely at his expense.

But when the first flush of it was over, and Felix had accepted, calling him a good little chap and saying how much he would miss him, poor Tommy grew apprehensive. In spite of all his recent experience, he had but the vaguest idea of what such a meal was going to cost. All that remained of his windfall from the English Press was seventeen pounds. The new gray suit had been shockingly dear, and he himself would have preferred another, at half the price and in a beautiful sea-colored gabardine, but Felix for once had been immovable. "No, *no,* you little old funny," was all he would say. Lying in Tommy's drawer was the sweetest, kindest letter he had ever written, describing to his mother the great good fortune that had befallen him, promising her support in the days to come and asking her to accept at once, in earnest of his filial devotion—"no less profound for having so long remained unexpressed"—the sum of ten pounds; and there in his drawer it would have to stop for the present. Seventeen pounds less whatever this wild invitation would swallow had to see him out until he was paid at the end of his first month, and he was not even due to start work for another five days. As he dwelt bitterly on these facts, he could have kicked himself for his folly.

Now the day of the luncheon had arrived and he felt the absurdity of his position more than ever. There was something grotesque in the very offering of a meal to a man as rich as Felix was, something abhorrent to nature. It was jarring to himself as well, for by temperament and conviction he was a guest. While he reflected, his sense of grievance returned and he began to feel that Felix had tricked him into it, playing on his simplicity with all that extravagant fuss about his aunt. Tommy could imagine no pleasanter thing than a long visit to a rich lady in Torremolinos, and he suspected Felix of showing off. His thoughts then turned to the particular lady in question and to the pernicious letter in *The Times* that had wrought such fearful havoc; and he began to think that the Horniman family was thoroughly detrimental. Next he remembered with a stab of pain that Felix had never so much as hinted at any future meeting, or even asked him to keep in touch; there came into his mind with horrid distinctness, as always happened when his spirits were low, the words Felix had uttered before he mounted the stallion at Topsy's; and what with one thing and another and with the grief it caused him to think of seeing the merry, heartless creature no more, he was in half a mind to ring him up and say he was ill.

No sooner had the thought come into his mind than he repented of it, aware that Felix would see through him at once. The steely shrewdness behind the levity had made itself felt before. He began instead to wheedle himself into a cheerful mood by a recital of his blessings. He had a fine new job and a find new suit and at least some money in his pocket; and if the worst came to the worst his fine new friends would probably lend him some more, or put him in the way of earning it. With the loss of public interest in the Lafuente, now that it was not to become an issue, had come a dismal falling-off of interest in its captor, as he could not but recognize from the changed demeanor of those who so lately had fawned upon him; but he continued to look on his feat as a potential gold mine and had laid in a mound of paper and several pens against the day when the rush of orders should begin. Or why should he not after all get his due reward from that journalist, the one to whom despite the appearances he had *really* sold his exclusive story? He already had telephoned once to the man, stating his own, clearly reasoned view of the situation, and had been appalled by the venom of his reply; but there was nothing to prevent his trying again.

So earnestly, wisely and lovingly did he admonish himself in this way, that his spirits soon began to revive; and a prolonged study of himself in the looking glass completed the cure. He thought suddenly that he was handsomer now than he ever had been. It was not merely the effect of the smart new clothes but also that, eating regularly at Felix's expense, he had put on flesh and, driving with Felix about the country, he had acquired a healthy tan. The reflection in the glass was smiling appreciatively at him, and he decided to go into town at once and stroll about where others could see him until it was time to meet Mr. Horniman.

When he got out of the bus at Dawson Street, however, he noticed that something was up. The Guard on duty at the bottom of Grafton Street was waving his arms as if distracted, and a small crowd on the pavement near by were craning their necks for a view of something or other that approached from the direction of Trinity College. Presently there came the hollow beat of drums, and around the corner shambled the front ranks of a procession of National students, each bearing a placard at the top of a pole. Abolish the Secret Police! said one; and, Worse Than Beria! stated the next. Thumbscrews Now? sharply queried a third; and there was a forest of others, each expressing sentiments of a similar nature in an equally pithy style. Now and again as they shuffled along, the pale, intense young men would sheepishly call these slogans out to the amused or indifferent spectators.

To one of Tommy's political discernment the grounds for the demonstration were immediately plain. For some time past an ugly spirit had been stirring in the Irish Republic. While the heroes of the past were still revered as such, those who followed in their steps today and did exactly the same things were not infrequently clapped into jail. A flagrant example of this new order had taken place a few days before, undoubtedly giving rise to this spirited protest on the part of uncorrupted Irish youth.

Early one morning a score or so of young patriots had been quietly carrying out a little machine-gun practice in a secluded part of the Wicklow Mountains, when suddenly, and without fair warning, they had been surrounded by Guards and borne away to the Bridewell. The plea of their captain that he had to go on to a Mass for the repose of his mother's soul was ignored. The victims had all appeared the following day on obviously trumped-up charges, and had been remanded in custody at the urgent request of the superintendent; and this individual it plainly was who had called forth the unfavorable comparison with the notorious Russian.

Tommy watched the students come on with strangely mingled feelings. In his new position of civic responsibility, he could not but realize that such doings might get the country a bad name, with probable ill effects to the tourist trade. "Come to Lovely Erin" was all very well, but if lovely Erin were bristling with machine guns and bombs, a great many timid souls whose money was urgently needed might prefer to remain at home. Yet his own revolutionary past was not so dead in him that he could look on such activities unmoved; and accordingly he went over the road and stood waiting for the procession to go by.

What followed was not in the very least to his liking. The leader of the students, a spotty, bespectacled youth who had been glancing furtively about him in the extremes of self-consciousness and cursing the hour in which he had ever agreed to come, at once recognized the national hero and acclaimed him with a ringing shout of "O'Driscoll! It's himself!" Those behind him took up the cry, which traveled slowly down to the tail of the column until every man jack of them was bawling "O'Driscoll!" at the top of his lungs. Tommy was already shivering with fright lest someone important should happen to come along and see it, when, to his absolute horror, the leader shouted, "March with us, O'Driscoll! March with us for a free Ireland!"

"Ah no, ah no!" the hero muttered, anxiously backing away.

"Come on, there's the lad! Irish students salute you and look to you!"

"O'Driscoll, march with us for a free Ireland!" now began a noisy chant from the rear.

Nothing would have pleased him more than to knock all their stupid heads together; but, like all established patriots, he was terrified of appearing less patriotic than somebody else. He thought, too, that if public disturbance and scandal were to be avoided, it would be wise to give in. From the route the boys had taken he judged that they meant to proceed to the Dáil, where he hoped that someone in authority would persuade them to go home and he could quietly slip away. He therefore fell in beside the leader, marching along with the best grace he could find, and when they reached Kildare Street, made as if to turn up into it.

"Not there! Not yet!" commanded the leader. This valuable new recruit to the cause had made another man of him. "The British Embassy first."

"The British Embassy!" echoed Tommy in ever-deepening dismay. "Why, this is an Irish affair!"

"England's hand is behind it," the patriot revealed. "Puppets! That's all our politicians are today. Down with the secret police!" he trumpeted over the road to a mild-looking man who stood in the doorway of a bookshop.

"Oh, and is that the size of it, Mr. Murphy?" came the reply. "And me thinking you'd come to pay your bill!"

Appreciative chuckles arose among the bystanders.

"Beneath our notice," Mr. Murphy confided to Tommy, throwing his meager shoulders back. "Miserable West Britons, the lot of them. Beria's ghost walks again in Ireland!" he boomed.

Oh—all patriots! thought Tommy in bitter disgust. By now he was certain he would not care if every single member of Sinn Fein were cast into jail and kept there. Why these crusading fanatics must always involve peaceable men in their horseplay was quite beyond him. Now they were trudging across the lower end of Merrion Square and in a minute or two they would reach the Embassy, where, as he knew, a Guard was usually posted. Suppose now there were an incident and he were arrested? No man, he told himself, was readier to run hazards for Ireland on alien soil, as he had amply shown; but where was the charm, the poetry, the romance of being arrested in Dublin? And what would become of his fine new appointment then? And what would Mr. Davenport say? For

Tommy was determined to cultivate Mr. Davenport as a useful connection when Felix had disappeared.

"Right wheel!" ordered the leader as they came up to the corner of the Square; and then, unexpectedly, in a high, agitated voice, "Halt! Halt! Halt!" The column obeyed in some confusion and, as they could not see what was happening, began to mutter among themselves. Tommy's view was all too clear, however, and he stared ahead of him in blank amazement.

The scene in progress some little distance away was like something out of a dream. To begin with, there was a great ragged hole in one of the Embassy windows. There were half a dozen Guards at least instead of the usual solitary one; two of these held an old man firmly between them while another examined a strip of what appeared to be leopard skin, and a fourth loosely swung by its tail an object that strangely resembled a cat. Mr. Davenport stood on the steps, his face white and working, and his hair on end; and beside him was Felix, unruffled and smiling as ever, endeavoring to calm him down. But it was the elderly captive, struggling and complaining in the arms of the stolid Guards, that riveted Tommy's horrified gaze. That noble head, that silver mane—surely . . . ? But it could not be. The prisoner's voice now lifted itself in mingled entreaty and objurgation, a rich, deep, rumbling, unforgettable voice; could there be two such voices in the world? Tommy stood there paralyzed in consternation, his brain incapable of a single thought.

"Who's the old fellow they've got there?" queried someone in the rank behind. "Will we rush them?"

"Ah, wait now, boys," Mr. Murphy begged them, shakily. His new confidence had promptly subsided at the sight of the blue uniform. "They'd be too many for us."

"God almighty, Joe! And we're seventy strong!"

"But they're all heavily armed and utterly ruthless," improvised the trembling commander. "And what would your parents think of me, if someone got hurt? And the University wouldn't like it at all. We've the future to think of, all the same."

"Ah, Joe! Are you a man at all?"

Other protests came from the rear, but there was a notable lack of fire about them, and in any case the Guards settled the argument now by bundling the old man into a car and driving away at high speed.

The leader gave a loud sigh of relief. "Please God the day shall come when scenes like that are witnessed in Ireland no more," he said fervently. "Right about turn! We'll go to the Dáil; it might be a little awkward here. They've trouble enough, and we should only be in the way."

Now that all chance of action was gone, the majority of the demonstrators proved to have been strongly in favor of it; but they obediently wheeled about and trailed away in the opposite direction.

"There went the greatest of living Irishmen!" Tommy said to Mr. Murphy, in a voice that shook with emotion and contempt. "I have the honor to wish you good day." And, raising one hand in ironic salute, he swept off in majesty toward the Embassy, while the other man gazed after him in bewilderment for a moment or two before running to catch up with his flock.

The outraged hero was by no means sure of the truth of what he had just said. Excited by the drama on the Embassy steps, he had felt an overpowering need to strike an attitude of some kind; and, further, he was glad of any excuse to separate himself from the demonstration. On the whole he thought, he wanted to think, that he was mistaken. The colossal, imperial dignity of the man he had known was not in keeping with the shouts and gesticulations of the Guards' unhappy victim. But if he were right, and if he had stood helplessly by while the greatest of living Irishmen was carried away without raising a finger to help him? You couldn't have done much by yourself, one of his two minds consoled the other. It was the students he should blame, not himself. They would overthrow the power of England, if you don't mind, and they ran from a couple of Civic Guards! They had "the future to think of, all the same"! Could there exist a mentality more abject, more ignoble? That famous description of Dublin as a "city of genteel dastards and bellowing slaves" came into his mind and struck him as equally accurate now as it ever had been.

" 'Shall we be thus forever?' " he groaned aloud.

Felix now disappeared into the Embassy, leading Mr. Davenport by the arm and talking in a gentle, soothing way as if to a terrified child. Tommy began to pace up and down outside, his brain still whirling with indignation, until one of the remaining Guards came up and gruffly asked what he wanted.

"I am waiting for Mr. Horniman," Tommy replied in all the dignity of his new clothes and with a passable imitation of an English accent.

"And who's Mr. Horniman?"

"He is the gentleman who has just gone inside with Mr. Davenport," was the lofty reply. "He is lunching with me. At Jammet's."

"Oh, is that right?"

"What has been happening here, if I may ask?"

"Nothing," said the Guard rudely and finally. "Nothing at all."

Presently Felix emerged onto the steps again, wreathed in smiles. "Why, Tommy, dear thing, what brings you here? How we do run into each other!" he sang out at once. Whatever indignity his Embassy might have undergone, it had apparently not affected his buoyant spirits. "Come along. The old bus is just round the corner. Oh, what a wonderful country Ireland is! I'm almost sorry to leave. But the dear old fellow went a little too far. Did you see the hole in the window? I'm afraid they'll hang him now."

"Hang him!" Tommy screamed.

"Now now, not literally, you know. But it doesn't really do to hurl the Ambassador's Book through the window, whatever the provocation. Poor old Freddie! It must have been a brainstorm, or something of that kind."

"Poor old Freddie? But the other! Felix, who was the other?" Tommy panted. "I only saw you all from the end of the street and I . . . It's almost impossible but . . . I almost thought it was the Bombardier!"

"Not a bit of it," Felix assured him briskly. "That was a tedious old crackpot who's been baiting Freddie for months. Every time he comes round there's a new bat in his belfry, and today he's in Mau Mau. It's extraordinary, if you think of it, the trouble he takes. He'd even bought a yard or so of fur fabric to look like a leopard skin! Somehow or other he sneaked into the Embassy, and they found him busy nailing a horridly dead cat to Freddie's door. Well, nothing very much in that and they could easily have hushed it up in the normal way (his brother's a Bishop), but old Freddie suddenly went off his nut. I'd just dropped in to say a fond farewell, and before I could stop him he charged out of the room like a wounded buffalo, picked up the holy Book, and crash! I don't remember him at school as so very highly strung; a placid child, he always seemed. Well, the shindy brought the peelers running, shouting to their chums as they came, and the fat was in the fire. But it's the deuce of a worry, you know. Freddie isn't at all himself. I realized he wasn't the first moment I saw him here. He's been taking Ireland seriously, I fear, and of course no good ever came of that."

"Oh. Oh, was that all?" was the only comment that Tommy made to this singular narrative. His relief was such that he allowed Felix's last remark to go by unchallenged. That vivid, that brilliant, imagination of his had merely been up to its tricks again and now the horror had passed away, leaving his heart full of peace. Suddenly he became aware for the first time of a change that gradually had taken place in himself. He no longer really wished to see the Bombardier again. To know him had been a privilege, and to serve under him had brought rewards beyond anything that could have been hoped for; but Tommy preferred he should now remain as a beautiful and inspiring memory. The young hero was dedicated henceforth to a service no less exacting but different altogether in kind.

He looked at the beautiful heads of the Wicklow Hills appearing blue in a gap between the rosy houses, and at the shrubs and flowers in the Square, and the handsome buildings beyond, all glowing in the gentle Dublin light; and all at once he was filled with a wild exhilaration as if he were floating miles from anywhere in oceans of spiritual bliss.

"Bless the boy! I declare he's dreaming again."

"Oh, Felix, I am so happy," he said incoherently. "I never felt anything like it before. I believe I'm undergoing a mystical experience, like the saints."

"Mystical experience, my Aunt Rosemary," Felix chuckled. "Your life is before you, you are not married, we're off to an excellent lunch, you're looking as smart as a film star, *and* you're the coming man in the Irish tourist trade. Mystical experiences are invariably founded on satisfactory material conditions."

"Ah, Felix," said Tommy with tender reproach, "that's the Englishman in you talking. You know I don't like to hear it. We know better in Ireland, thank God. That's why we've always been missionaries, and that's why the tourist trade is so important. You don't suppose I'd take this on just for the money? Once the world gets to know us and learns our way of life, they will see what is lacking in their own. I'd be so delighted, Felix," he went on, laying a hand on Felix's arm and looking wistfully into his face, "if I could think you'd learned to see our point of view a little better just through knowing me."

"Oh, I have, I promise you," Felix assured him, very gravely indeed.

Tommy gave his happy little sigh. "Come now. I'll take you to lunch," he said in a faraway voice.

"Nonsense. I'm going to take you," Felix replied as he got into the Daimler. "It's my last day, much too late for innovations. God help us! He's off again."

For Tommy was standing motionless on the curb and smiling vacantly like a loon, lost to the world around him and sunk in his dreams.

ABOUT THE AUTHOR

HONOR TRACY started writing after the war, when she was living in Dublin. In Ireland she was associated with an Irish literary review edited by Sean O'Faolain. She also wrote short stories and articles for English and American periodicals.

Miss Tracy has had three earlier books published in England—two nonfiction books on Japan and Ireland, and a short novel, *The Deserters*.

She wrote *The Straight and Narrow Path*, a modern classic, in Italy in the fall of 1954, while recovering from a long illness. *Silk Hats and No Breakfast* is her account of her travels in Spain, where she spent the summer of 1955.

THE PROSPECTS ARE PLEASING is a return to the locale and to the comic manner of *The Straight and Narrow Path*.